For all of her tough exterior, there was a softness in this woman that longed to come out; Sterling wanted to be the man to release it.

What kind of man had her husband been? Sterling wondered for the umpteenth time. It was clear that her ex-husband still had some kind of hold on Ann Marie. Was her reaction to the man simply one of old memories and bad vibes, or did she still care about him?

Sterling walked into the living room and saw Ann Marie standing in front of the windows. She looked so tiny and vulnerable. He decided there and then that he would make it his business to wipe her ex-husband out of her mind and, if need be, out of her heart for good.

"Dinner is served, madam," he said in a very bad British accent.

Ann Marie turned a gentle smile on her face. Sterling's insides shook just a little. Yes, he was going to make her forget.

DONNA HILL

began her novel-writing career in 1990. Since that time she's had more than forty titles in print, including full-length novels and novellas. Two of her novels and one novella were adapted for television. She has won numerous awards for her work. She is also the editor of five novels, two of which were nominated for awards. She easily moves from romance to erotica, horror, comedy and women's fiction. She was the first recipient of the Trailblazer Award and currently teaches writing at the Frederick Douglass Creative Arts Center. Donna lives in Brooklyn with her family. Visit her Web site at www.donnahill.com.

DONNA HILL
Saving All My
Lovin'

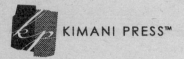 KIMANI PRESS™

ISBN-13: 978-1-58314-786-3
ISBN-10:   1-58314-786-1

SAVING ALL MY LOVIN'

www.kimanipress.com

Printed in U.S.A.

Dear Reader,

Thanks for joining the ladies once again as they prove that the "forties are fabulous!"

Having the opportunity to write the PAUSE FOR MEN series allows me to explore all the aspects of my characters— Barbara, Ann Marie, Stephanie and Elizabeth—and to find new and exciting romantic adventures for them to embark upon. The real treat is to be able to showcase mature women and kick to the curb the notion that young women have all the fun.

Although my ladies do have "drama" to deal with, they find a way to make it all work out.

Stay tuned for *If I Were Your Woman* (Kimani Romance, February 2007), which will feature Stephanie and Tony, the decisions they must make and the obstacles that they must overcome. The other ladies will definitely be there to support Stephanie as all four women share an ever-changing future filled with adventure!

Until next time,

Donna

Chapter 1

Ann Marie's feet were killing her. She'd been hoofing it around on those three-inch stilettos for what felt like an eternity. What she wouldn't give to add a couple of natural inches to her barely-beyond-five-foot height. But the agony was worth every wincing moment. The grand opening of Pause for Men was a phenomenal success.

She smiled to herself as she looked around while the last of the support staff finished cleaning up. She'd decided to stay behind until the cleanup was completed while her friends and business partners called it a night. Barbara, newly engaged and sporting a blinding diamond ring had gone on home with her young buck Michael. Steph left with her shoes in one hand and her other held by her new beau Tony. She'd caught a glimpse of Ellie tiptoeing away with her man Ron to her new apartment on the top floor of the brownstone.

She plopped down at the makeshift bar, nursing the watery remnants of her cosmopolitan. They'd done good. And it seemed as though all the unlikely folks had someone to go home to except for her. She couldn't ever remember going home alone. Funny, how life does a three-sixty and catches you unawares. Less than six months ago, she had her own man Phil. Then her grown, married daughter Raquel pops back into her life, moves in and everything that she'd taken for granted came undone.

To add complications to her life, Terrance Bishop had reappeared, found her and Raquel after more than two decades. *Terrance.* God she could still see his face as if it were only yesterday. She had yet to tell Raquel that Terrance was coming to New York and wanted to see them both.

She tugged on her bottom lip with her teeth, deep in the clutches of her dilemma. Although she'd reluctantly agreed to see him, she didn't know if that's what she really wanted. The kind of physical and emotional power Terrance had over her... She shivered just a little. Well, she didn't know if she could handle it, or if she wanted to.

Terrance Bishop: sexy, handsome, wealthy Island playboy; her husband, her daughter's father, her past. Her future?

She'd been barely sixteen when she was sent by her mother to live in the Bishop household. Terrance was the oldest of four and the only boy; doted on by his parents and worshipped by his sisters. He was ten years older than Ann Marie—a big man in stature and in the parish of St. Ann in Jamaica, West Indies where he followed in the footsteps of his father Cyril in the police department.

Her mother felt that Ann Marie was woman enough to be on her own, take care of her own man. Cyril wanted his son to settle down and Ann Marie's mother wanted her daughter out of her house. The agreement suited both parents. So Ann Marie and Terrance were married, and by the time Ann Marie was seventeen she was pregnant with Raquel.

Ann Marie was a virgin when she filled Terrance's marital bed both physically and emotionally, naïve to the ways of the world and the ways of men and women. Terrance on the other hand felt neither obligation nor fidelity in his marriage and continued with his playboy ways. Not even the birth of his beautiful daughter changed or slowed him down or kept the numerous women from calling, knocking on their door or snickering at her when she went into town to shop.

She stayed as long as she could. Two long, life-altering years before she fled to New York without a word to anyone. She'd been here ever since.

Ann Marie put her glass down on the counter and pushed herself up from her perch at the bar. That was then. She was a big woman now, not the cowering, innocent young thing that Terrance once knew. She could handle him now—him and her emotions.

"We're all done, ma'am."

Ann Marie looked across the wide, sparkling wood floor. The three young women they'd hired to help serve and clean up stood in a row. Ann Marie smiled, picked up her purse and approached them.

"Thank you all, on behalf of myself and the other owners. You did a wonderful job." She handed each of them an envelope with their payment for the night.

They smiled brightly, murmured their thanks and bounced out as if they'd just gotten up for the day. Ann Marie shook her head and chuckled. Youth, she thought. She took one last look around, shut off the lights and walked out, locking the front door behind her. She pulled in a big lungful of air and glanced skyward. The heavens were clear. The moon making its descent behind a bouquet of white cotton had an orange tinge to its edges. It was going to be a hot one tomorrow.

"Wonderful event tonight."

She jumped, startled by the voice coming from behind her.

"Sorry, I didn't mean to scare you."

She stole a glance over her shoulder and looked up, clutching her purse to her chest. Her heart slowed then picked up its pace when the voice became a body.

He was dressed in what she knew was an expensive suit, tailored to fit in a midnight blue. The stark white shirt against his milk chocolate skin made her instinctively lick her lips and the barely there scent of his cologne teased and cajoled.

"I saw you earlier. I wanted to introduce myself but you were very busy." One hand was in his pants pocket, the other at his side.

Her good sense and her voice had apparently stayed behind in the brownstone. She couldn't think of one thing to say.

His right brow rose. "Are you okay?" He looked around then back at her.

Ann Marie swallowed. "Yes. You…surprised me, that's all."

"Sterling Chambers." He stuck out his hand.

Ann Marie stared at it and finally figured out why he was pointing it at her. She placed her hand in his. "Ann Marie."

"Nice to *finally* meet you." He chuckled softly and the light from the moon bounced off his eyes.

"You were at the event tonight?" *How in the hell could she have missed him?*

He nodded. "Yep. It's quite a place. I actually signed up."

Her stomach did a little flip.

"What role did you play in it all? I got the impression that you were an important part of the evening, the way you were keeping people in line and welcoming the guests."

She felt her cheeks grow hot, thankful for the darkness. "I'm one of the co-owners, actually."

"I'm impressed." He pulled in a breath. "Listen, it's late and I know you must be beat. I wish we could have met earlier. I should let you go."

Was he leaving? Just like that?

He reached into the inside breast pocket of his suit jacket and pulled out a card. He handed it to her. "Maybe you can give me a call sometime and we can meet in the daylight." He smiled.

Oddly relieved, Ann Marie took the card. *Sterling Chambers, Esq*. She glanced up at him. "Lawyer?"

"Something like that."

She tucked the card into her purse. "Nice to meet you."

"You too."

She looked at him for a moment then turned and walked toward her car several feet away.

Raquel was fast asleep on the couch when Ann Marie came in. She took off her shoes and crept into the house, careful not to wake her.

Once inside her room, she quickly got undressed and washed the makeup from her face. Before getting into bed, she emptied her purse on top of her dresser.

Sterling's card was on top of the silver compact. She picked it up, ran her finger across the slightly raised black letters. So he'd been watching her. If only she'd known. Her smile was wicked.

She sighed and put the card down. Well, if he was for real, his name would be on the new members list. She'd find out soon enough. Tomorrow was the first official day of business.

She'd get *her* rest tonight. She wasn't too sure about her girlfriends, though. She got in bed and turned out the light.

Hmm, it had been months since she'd had sex. She flopped over onto her side, curled into a fetal position. Who would have ever thought that Ann Marie Dennis would be jealous that her friends were getting some and she wasn't?

She pounded the pillow with her fist and forced her eyes closed. This drought had to end soon.

Chapter 2

Pause was scheduled to open for official business at one o'clock. The girls all promised to be there by eleven, even Barbara. She'd taken a week's vacation from her job as a rehab specialist at the hospital to see Pause through the first few days.

Elizabeth was sitting behind the reception counter turning on the computer when Ann Marie arrived.

"Hey. You're really early." Elizabeth looked at the wall clock above the juice machine. "Great night last night, huh?"

"It sure was." Ann Marie took a seat at the reception counter. She leaned toward Elizabeth. "So…how was it, chile?"

Elizabeth's saffron complexion glowed crimson. "How…was w-hat?"

Ann Marie pursed her lips. "The boom-boom." She grinned.

"Ann Marie!" she hissed between her teeth as if there was someone else around to hear them. "That's private."

Ann Marie stretched out the top half of her body across the counter and laid her head down. "Can't I live vicariously through you?"

"What?" Elizabeth started to laugh. "You? You have got to be kidding."

"Me stuff gon' dry up and blow away."

Elizabeth covered her mouth and howled with laughter. "It can't be that bad," she sputtered over her chuckles.

Ann Marie partially lifted her head and turned dark eyes on Elizabeth. "Worse."

"Good morning partners," Barbara sang, sailing through the door. Stephanie was right behind her.

"Hey everybody." Stephanie sat down next to Ann Marie. "Too many drinks last night?" She lowered her head to meet Ann Marie at eye level.

"She says she's all dried up," Elizabeth said.

Barbara and Stephanie looked at each other in

a millisecond of confusion. Then it hit them simultaneously.

"Ooooh."

Barbara put her arm around Ann Marie's shoulders. "It'll be all right girl. The right man will come along before you know it."

"Easy for you to say," she grumbled. "You got a man/child and you been to the Promised Land."

The trio broke up laughing and even Ann Marie had to join in.

"You definitely have blossomed," Stephanie said to Barbara. "You look happy."

Barbara blushed. "I am happy." She turned her smile on each of her friends. "And I have to thank you all for that."

"Us?" Elizabeth asked.

Barbara nodded. "Yes, if you all hadn't convinced me to take a chance on Michael..." She shrugged.

Stephanie placed her hand on Barbara's shoulder and angled her head to the side. "What red-blooded, healthy woman wouldn't take a chance on a fine young thing like Michael? And he has money too! Girl you got it made." She waved her hand.

"Look who's talking," Elizabeth piped in. "You got a little more than lucky with Tony."

Stephanie grinned. She tossed her weave over

her shoulder. "He definitely has potential." She turned to Elizabeth, her eyes narrowing. "Did, uh, you and Ron christen your new bedroom last night?"

Elizabeth sucked in a gasp as all eyes turned on her. She lowered her gaze then looked up. "Yes! Yes! Yes!" Her smile showcased every tooth in her mouth.

"I take that as a yes," Barbara said and they all high fived, except for Ann Marie who'd retreated to a stool at the end of the counter.

She looked smaller than usual, childlike almost with her clear complexion and hair pulled back into a ponytail. Her diminutive body was clad in a form-fitting baby pink velour tracksuit and for once she didn't have on heels. She was staring off into space and had to clear her head of its turmoil when she realized her three friends were standing in front of her.

"What's up Ann?" Barbara, ever the mother and counsel asked in a soft voice.

Ann Marie sighed. "I feel alone. For the first time in years, me actually feel alone." Her eyes suddenly filled, taking the trio by such surprise they didn't know how to respond.

Tears were usually the domain of Elizabeth. Ann Marie, on the other hand, was notorious for her sharp tongue and indifferent attitude. This was a side they'd never seen.

Ann Marie sniffed hard then began fumbling in her bag for a tissue. She wiped her eyes and nose then straightened her shoulders. Drawing in a breath of resolve she looked her friends in the eye. "PM fuckin' S." She snickered. "That's all. So don't be gettin' all gooey-eyes wit me. I'm still a bitch." She sniffed again. "So are we here to work or hang out at the bar?"

Everyone's smiles returned. That was the Ann Marie they recognized.

"Well, I'm going to do some Web searching and see how much coverage we got then make some calls," Stephanie said, easily slipping on her PR hat.

"I'm going to check the equipment and make sure all the supplies are in place," Barbara said. "As much as I'm going to love running my hands over all those male bodies, we're going to have to get some other therapists in here other than me. If last night was any indication of the client load, we're going to be busy."

Elizabeth nodded, tugging on her bottom lip with her teeth, deep in thought. "I'll put together a list of potential positions and what qualifications we're looking for and then we can all review it later on today."

"Sounds good," Ann Marie said. "I'll work on the roster for the new clientele." And of course she'd check out Mr. Chambers in the process. She headed over to the check-in station, a horseshoe shaped black ceramic table topped with two flat-screen computer monitors, a multi-line phone, rolodex, fax and credit card machine. Beneath the counter was a three-drawer rollaway file cabinet that would contain the hardcopies of client information.

She flipped open the guest book from the previous night and one by one began to scroll through the names. There it was on page three: *Sterling Chambers*. Ann Marie smiled. She turned on the computer and opened up the Member database. She clicked on the Search field and typed in Sterling's name. In a blink of an eye, all of his basic information appeared on the screen: address, phone number, cell and how he paid—*American Express Platinum*. When the details were complete she'd know his exact height, weight, general physical health, eye color and emergency contact name—hopefully not a spouse. This whole spa thing for men could really turn into a goldmine. It would be raining men nonstop.

"Glad to see you smiling." Barbara set a stack of white towels on the counter.

Ann Marie's head snapped up. "Oh." She

clicked off from the screen. "Yeah, having one of those moments."

Barbara smiled. "Well, I better get set up. The doors will be opening soon." She walked off.

Barbara was the one constant in the group that everyone seemed to turn to, even her. But this time she kept her little secret to herself. They'd all agreed when they'd decided on this little venture that it was only to look and not touch, to fantasize, not act on the fantasy. So the last thing she wanted her friends to think was that she was desperate and using the spa as a dating service.

The doorbell rang. Ann Marie's heart jumped in her chest. She watched Elizabeth go to the door, held her breath and released it with a disappointed sigh when Dawne, Elizabeth's daughter came in laden with trays of food.

"Hi!" she called out. "I'll take these to the kitchen. Desiree is bringing the rest." She hurried off. Desiree soon followed pushing a cart of canisters of their specially made health juices. Having two daughters that owned their own health food restaurant was paying off already.

Before long they were all too busy to think straight. Within the first two hours twenty men had come through the door. Some had come to the grand opening the night before; others were referred by those who did.

Ann Marie worked the front desk with Elizabeth registering the men and giving them a quick tour of the facilities. Everyone wanted a massage. Lucky Barbara, she thought as she keyed in the information on yet another newcomer. Her fingers felt as if they would fall off and it had barely been four hours. If this many men were available during the day what would happen after the regular work day was over?

As she worked on printing out hardcopies of client records to be filed away, Raquel walked in.

Ann Marie stopped what she was doing and stood, stretching her stiff back in the process. She would need one of Barbara's massages at this rate.

"This is a surprise. I wasn't expecting you."

Raquel's heavenly brown eyes were red-rimmed. Ann Marie frowned. "Chile what's wrong?"

"Why don't you tell me, mama?"

"Look, I'm working. Me no have time for games."

"It's not me playing games."

Ann Marie huffed and came from around the counter. She grabbed Raquel by the arm and spoke in a harsh whisper.

"I don't know what burr you got up your butt, but you best change your tone and quick. Me your mum, not some friend on the street."

"Really? Then why don't you treat me like I'm your daughter?" Tears splashed over her cheeks.

Ann Marie looked around to see if anyone was paying attention to the drama unfolding. They all were too busy.

"Come with me." She pulled Raquel across the room and down the corridor to the back office. She pushed the door open without knocking.

Stephanie dribbled water down the front of her blouse. "What the..." She caught the look of fire in Ann Marie's eyes. And who could miss the tear-streaked face of Raquel? "Uh, I was just leaving. Looks like a mother daughter moment." She picked up the file she was working on, gave them both one last look and eased out, shutting the door softly behind her.

Ann Marie whirled on Raquel, her hands planted firmly on her hips. "You want to explain what your problem is?"

Raquel drew in two short, shuddering breaths trying to collect herself. "I was on my way out, to see about a consulting job and the phone rang."

Ann Marie suddenly felt queasy.

"Why didn't you tell me?"

"What?" she croaked without the bravado of moments ago.

"About my father! About the fact that he's recently been in touch with you. About the fact that he's planning on coming to the States and wants to see me. About the fact that you're still married to him!"

Ann Marie lowered her defiant gaze and stepped away from her accuser. She drew in a breath and straightened to her five-foot-two-inch height. She turned to Raquel.

"I have reasons which you can't begin to understand."

"Tell me."

"No! It is my business." She poked at her chest. "You know nothing of the man. But I do." A shiver ran through her. "I left him and Jamaica for good reasons. To protect me and you."

"From my father?" she asked in disbelief.

Ann Marie swallowed. "From a life I could no longer endure."

"You're not making sense. What happened in Jamaica between you and my father?"

"I won't discuss it with you Raquel. Now or ever."

Raquel snickered. "That's so like you. You have to be in control. Anything to hurt me and push me away." Her voice shattered like a glass tossed against concrete. "And I thought we were finally getting to a place where we could be mother and daughter—after all these years." She slowly shook her head, sniffed hard and wiped the tears away with the back of her hand. She looked Ann Marie square in the eyes. "Nothing has changed, Mama. Least of all you."

She spun away, nearly tore the door from its frame and stormed out. She stopped halfway and tossed over her shoulder, "He said to let you know that business is holding up his plans. He'll be here at the end of next month. And I plan to see him when he arrives." She pushed her way passed several clients and disappeared from Ann Marie's view.

Ann Marie slowly lowered herself into the swivel chair. In control? When it came to Terrance Bishop control never entered the equation. She covered her face with her hands and for the second time in one day she wept.

Activity at the open door drew up her head from her hands. Barbara, Stephanie and Ellie stood on the threshold. They all tried to get through the door at once. If she didn't feel so god-awful she'd laugh at the spectacle.

She quickly wiped her eyes, but not quickly enough.

"What is going on?" Barbara asked.

"Raquel went tearing out of here like her butt was on fire," Stephanie added.

"Are you crying?" Ellie asked in amazement.

The trio hovered over her like moths to a flame. She looked from one concerned face to another, which only caused another fresh set of tears to flow.

Barbara knelt down beside her and drew her close. "Ssssh," she soothed. "Whatever it is, it will be all right."

"We're here for you," Stephanie offered.

"Absolutely," Ellie added.

Stephanie sat on the edge of the desk. Ellie drew up a chair and took Ann Marie's hand, patting it gently.

"He—he spoke to her."

The trio looked at each other and then realization hit. All eyes widened simultaneously.

"Oh," they chorused.

"I take it you hadn't spoken to Raquel," Barbara said.

Ann Marie shook her head.

"How did he get your home number?" Stephanie asked.

Ann Marie swallowed. "Him a police officer. If he got me job number and address, the home number couldn't be hard to get."

"But after more than twenty years what made him resurface now?" Barbara asked.

The question sat in the room like rotten food. No one wanted to touch it.

Chapter 3

Somehow, Ann Marie managed to get through the rest of the day without any more outward displays of emotion and even put in a few hours of work at the real estate office. Work was the best cure. If she kept busy she wouldn't have to think and hopefully by the time she got home Raquel would be asleep.

She wasn't so lucky. Raquel was sitting in the living room waiting for her when she finally walked through the door.

"I wanted to wait until you got home to tell you that I was leaving." Raquel stood and that's when

Ann Marie noticed the suitcases neatly lined up near the couch.

Ann Marie lifted her chin. "Time you got back on your own two feet."

Raquel snorted her disgust. "Figured that's what you'd say." She picked up her two suitcases and approached her mother. "You know, most little girls want to grow up to be just like their mothers. I pray that I don't ever turn into the woman that you are." She brushed by Ann Marie and walked out the door that Ann Marie had never closed.

Ann Marie drew in a sharp, pain-filled breath when she heard the door slam shut.

On a night like tonight, with the day she'd had, she would have sought comfort in the arms of her man. But she didn't have one.   .

A lie, or at least the omission of the truth, lost Phil to her. A secret, or maybe it was a lie now, lost her daughter to her as well.

She'd been so good at keeping secrets. Only sharing parts of herself that she wanted the world to see—including her closest friends. Secrets had sustained her, helped her to believe that her reality wasn't true. Over the years she'd convinced herself that her life was perfect, just the way she wanted it. But there was a hole in her soul that she'd been unable to fill with men, work, fancy clothes, a good job. Nothing could stuff that gaping abyss.

She wanted to love and be loved but she didn't know how. At times she believed that she was saving all her love for the right time, the right person. When the ice between her and Raquel had finally been broken, she momentarily thought that perhaps the love she'd been seeking had been found.

But love was the great betrayer. She'd loved her mother. She'd loved her husband. She'd begun to allow herself to love her daughter. They all betrayed her. They took her fragile emotions and crushed them, believing that Ann Marie Dennis Bishop didn't need their love and affection. She was strong and independent.

She picked up a wine glass from the shelf of the étagère and threw it across the room. It smashed against the wall and cascaded into sparkling pieces.

What did they know? What did any of them know?

Barbara woke to the sound of a ringing telephone. She squinted at the digital clock on her bedside. 2:00 a.m. She groaned and fumbled for the phone.

"Hello," she answered her voice thick with sleep.

"Hey baby."

She blinked several times and turned on her

side, a soft smile forming around her mouth. "Hey babe, yourself. Is everything okay?"

"Yeah, everything is fine. I know it's late. But I'm just getting in. Listen, I want you to fly out to L.A. I'm going to be here for about a week and I want to show you off to the fellas."

Barbara pushed herself up into a half-sitting position and leaned on her elbow. "California?"

"Yeah, I'm doing a commercial before I head out to Florida with the rest of the team."

"Mike...I'd love to but—"

"No buts. When was the last time you took an all expense paid, spur of the moment trip?"

She giggled. "I can't say that I have."

"My point exactly. We could have some fun. You get to relax. I get to wine and dine you...and in between..."

She sighed as she imagined being in some fancy hotel with her rich and famous NBA fiancé, being courted around town in style. She'd definitely have some stories to tell the girls when she got back.

The girls. The spa. Her job.

"Mike, the spa just opened. We have our hands full. I mean today alone I must have done two dozen massages. We're already looking to hire staff."

He didn't respond.

"Mike?"

"Yeah, well, important things first."

"Don't be like that."

"Like what? Aggravated that you'd rather run your hands all over some other man rather than your own?"

She flinched away from the sharp edge of his tongue. "Michael! You know better than that. It's my job."

He muttered something she didn't quite catch.

"Do I tell you not to attend the after parties or sign autographs for the *sweet young things* that are all over you after a game?" She was wide awake now.

"That's different."

"Really?" Her sarcastic tone was lost on him.

"Look, forget it. It was a stupid idea. I just thought it would be fun for both of us."

Barbara squeezed her eyes shut against the sound of hurt and disappointment in his voice.

"I'll see if I can get rid of the airline tickets. Maybe one of my teammates can use them."

Tickets? He'd already bought her tickets? Guilt climbed on top of her chest and sat there tapping its foot.

She'd have to find a way to make it up to him.

"Mike…as soon as things settle down on this end and I can hire someone to take over for me at the spa…*and* I can give my job enough notice…I'd be happy to go anywhere in the world with you," she said in her most cajoling, please-understand tone.

He breathed heavily into the phone. "When we're married, you're not going to have to worry about any of this stuff."

"What do you mean?"

"I mean worrying about a job and obligations to other people. You'll have me and enough money to do what you want, when you want."

Concern nudged her. She jerked from it, frowned then swatted it away but it settled on the bed next to her and made itself comfortable, right next to her good sense.

She didn't like the feeling and it wasn't the first time it had reared its head when it came to Michael.

"Sounds like something we should really talk about when you're here in New York." She yawned, hoping the hint would get him off the phone. She wanted the call to end before something was said that couldn't be taken back.

"Yeah, you're right, baby. I shouldn't have put all this on you in the middle of the night. That was real selfish of me." His voice lowered to the deep timber that always left her weak. "I guess I'm missing you too much."

That tight spot in the center of her chest softened.

"You accept my apology?"

"Mike you have nothing to apologize for. It was a sweet offer. Really. And if it was any other time, I would go in a heartbeat."

He chuckled. "I know. Look, you get your beautiful self some rest. I'll try to call you tomorrow."

"When will you be back?"

"Not for a couple weeks. But if I can get away even for a weekend or overnight, I'll be there."

A hot flush filled her up. "I can't wait," she whispered.

"I love you."

"I love you, too."

"Night."

"Good night." Slowly she hung up the phone and tried to settle back down to sleep but doubt had joined concern and good sense in her bed and she barely had room to move.

There were things that troubled her about her relationship with Michael; little things that flared up unexpectedly, the little flashes of jealousy, the silences.

She flipped onto her side, couldn't get comfortable, kicked her unwanted guests onto the floor then lay spread-eagle in the bed.

It was late. She was awakened from a well-earned rest. She was making more out of things than necessary, worrying about nothing.

She stuck her left hand out in front of her. Even in the darkness of her bedroom the diamond sparkled, reminding her of her commitment to a man almost young enough to be her son.

She drew in a breath. It would work out. She deserved some happiness. It had been a long drought since she'd lost her husband Marvin and Michael made her feel alive again, reminded her that she was still a vibrant, sexy woman.

She turned back onto her side. Now that she had some room in the bed, she planned to get to sleep. But doubt, good sense and concern crept back beneath the sheets and spent the rest of the night.

Ann Marie spent a sleepless night as well. She'd told the girls the day before that she'd be unable to work at the spa as she had a long day at the real estate office, several meetings and a closing.

When she arrived at the office, thankfully, she was the only one there. She turned on the coffee pot and stood in front of it like a sentinel, waiting for it to perk. Funny, she thought absently, the coffeepot was a reflection of her life—sitting on a hot plate waiting to perk.

"Morning Ann Marie," Carol the new office assistant sang out.

Ann Marie turned away from staring at the pot. "Morning."

"You look a little tired. Long night?" She giggled in a way that would annoy the average person.

Inwardly Ann Marie rolled her eyes. "Something like that." She hadn't told anyone in the office about her new business venture, mainly because it was none of their business. And the less the staff knew about her private life the better. It was bad enough that Terrance had sent the flowers to her office, which caused all kinds of buzz and speculation.

"Out with the guy who sent the flowers?" she hedged.

Ann Marie snapped her head in Carol's direction. "I have two clients coming in, one at eleven and the other at one. Please make sure that their information is ready for me." She gave Carol the names of her clients, took the pot of coffee and poured herself a cup. She turned to Carol who stood there as if Ann Marie was still planning to tell her more about her private life.

Ann Marie arched a brow, stuck her arm out and dramatically examined her watch.

Carol finally got the hint. Ann Marie rolled her eyes in earnest and went to her cubicle.

The real estate office that she worked for was truly a high-end office, dealing only in luxury condos, commercial properties and brownstones, which had become the crown jewels of the marketplace. They had state of the art equipment, a designer's lounge area for clients, light refreshments and all of the agents had their own glass cubicles on two levels. The commissions that she raked in from sales put her solidly in the six-figure income bracket each year. If she wanted, she could leave New York at anytime and start a fresh life without a financial worry in the world.

Maybe that's what she needed to do—start over. Just pick up and leave all this crap behind. Go someplace where no one could find her. Maybe even change her name. There was nothing holding her here. She had no family—now with Raquel gone. She had no man. And…you could always make new friends.

She thought of Barbara, Stephanie and Ellie. They'd been her family, putting up with her bull for years. But even they couldn't give her what she needed.

Her desk phone rang. Absently she picked it up. "Ann Marie speaking."

"Did you get my message from our daughter?"

Her stomach did a slow somersault. "Yes," she choked out. "What do you want now, Terrance?" She gripped the edge of the desk.

"Nothing more than to hear your voice. Is that so wrong?"

"Very expensive call just to hear someone's voice."

"Money is not an issue. Never was. We had other problems—you and I."

"Oh, so you remember?"

"I was a fool, a young arrogant fool. But I've changed, Mari," he said, using his pet name for her.

Heat rushed to her head at the sound of the endearment. "Old dog as they say."

"I'm going to prove the saying wrong. You can teach this old dog new tricks." His voice lassóed around her. "I want you to teach me."

"It's over, Terrance."

"You're still my wife." The last two words tightened the rope around her neck, cut off her breathing.

"I'm busy Terrance. No time for your word games."

"It's not a game, Mari. I'm coming back for you. Believe that if you believe nothing else. And I will make you remember how good it was between us."

She slammed down the phone. Her hands were shaking. For several moments she sat there with her hand still locked on the receiver, unable to move. Her gaze rose upward and Carol was standing outside her cubicle staring at her.

Ann Marie drew in a breath, stood and tugged the hem of her waist length jacket then went to her door. She pulled it open.

"Yes!"

"Here are the files you asked for," she said, inching them toward Ann Marie as if handing off explosives.

Ann Marie swallowed. "Thank you," she murmured.

"Are you all right, Ms. Dennis?"

Ann Marie looked into Carol's eyes, and was stunned by what appeared to be real concern etched onto her acne-prone face.

Slowly Ann Marie nodded. "Yes, I'm fine," she said in a softer voice. "Thanks for asking." She took the files and turned away.

Ann Marie returned to her desk and eased her way down into her seat without collapsing.

How could she ever explain to anyone what Terrance did to her? Just his voice alone made her weak. Seeing him in her mind's eye made her hot with a need that had never been fully satisfied since she'd left him.

Yes, she'd played the role of the big woman in front of her friends. But with Terrance she was sixteen again, young, vulnerable and terribly in love with a man who only knew how to love himself.

He said he'd changed. She couldn't imagine that. But what if he had? What if he was the man she'd always wanted him to be? What then?

You're still my wife. The words echoed in her head like a shout tossed into the Grand Canyon. She had to make it stop. She couldn't lose her soul to Terrance Bishop again.

Chapter 4

Barbara, Ellie and Stephanie reviewed the write-up they'd put together to recruit staff. The day had been exhausting to say the least.

"Personally, Steph, I think you did too good of a job," Ellie moaned. "There was another write-up in the Style section of the *Times* today. And I got two calls this morning for a radio and a television interview."

"We could be moaning that the business was a flop," Barbara said, always practical. "So we really shouldn't complain."

"True, but we definitely have to get some

trained staff in here or they will be scraping us up off the floor," Ellie said.

"Not to change the subject from our successful endeavor, but has anyone heard from Ann Marie?" Stephanie looked at Barbara then Elizabeth. They both shook their heads no.

"In all the years I've known Ann Marie, I don't ever think I've seen her cry. She'd rather cut someone first," Elizabeth said, tongue in cheek.

"Yeah, me either," Barbara concurred. "I'm worried about her. She put on a good face about Terrance but she's truly shook. He must really be something to have put the mojo on Ann Marie."

"Not to mention the blowup between her and Raquel," Stephanie added. "I really thought they were going to make a go at it."

"Hmm," they murmured.

"So, what are we going to do?" Elizabeth asked.

"Sounds like our girl needs some sisterly intervention," Barbara said. "But first let's get this posting listed as soon as possible before *we* need the intervention."

"I'll put it up on *Craig's List* and see how that pans out," Stephanie said.

"And I'll post it on the hospital bulletin board," Barbara said.

They stood.

"So what time do we make this intervention?" Elizabeth asked.

"I'll make dinner and we can take it over to Ann Marie's," Barbara offered.

"I have a better idea. I'll call Dawne and Desiree and have them whip up something. No need for you to do any more work today, Barbara," Elizabeth said.

"Works for me." Barbara grinned.

"So let's meet at Ann Marie's about eight," Stephanie said.

They disbanded to handle the final business of the workday then headed out.

Ann Marie stuck her key in the lock of her apartment door and stepped inside. For a moment she expected to see Raquel sitting in the living room or to inhale the scent of dinner simmering on the stove.

The house was empty, silent and the only smell was the lingering fragrance of her body oil.

She shut the door, oddly disappointed. She didn't realize until that moment how accustomed she'd become to finding her daughter home when she arrived.

A sharp stab of angst caught her unawares. Maybe there was something she could have said to make Raquel stay, get her to understand.

On leaden legs she moved across the showcase

of a living room then on into her bedroom. She closed her door as if she half expected someone to suddenly walk in on her undressing. There was no one. The muscles of her throat tightened.

This was so unlike her, these bouts of tears and feeling sorry for herself. She was not some weak thing that could be bandied about by circumstance. She was the one who took circumstance by the balls and squeezed until she was satisfied.

Hadn't that been the way? Hadn't her resiliency, tough as nails, take no prisoner attitude been the ever recurring conversation piece at the weekly girls' soiree? She was the one who put the starch in Barbara's, Ellie's and Stephanie's backs. And now, she felt weak as a newborn, unable to stand on her own. And why? Because of a goddamn man!

She pulled her jacket off and tossed it haphazardly across the bed then stepped out of her shoes and left them right in the middle of the floor. She took off her blouse, unzipped her skirt and tossed both on top of her jacket.

What she needed was a stiff drink, at least that would have to suffice in lieu of something else stiff. She walked back into the living room in her Victoria's Secrets and fixed her herself a tall glass of Jamaican rum with barely a splash of Coke.

She gulped it down like a desert refugee left to bake in the sun then poured another. By the time she was halfway through her third drink and had moved away from the bar, the world had acquired a soft, warm, fuzzy feel around its edges.

Ann Marie smiled, stumbled over to the couch and plopped down with a flourish.

"The hell with you Terrance Bishop. You won't run your magic on me no more. Ya hear!" She jerked her glass into the air splashing some of the contents on her forehead. She giggled as she licked the sweet liquid that ran off the tip of her nose down to her lips.

She was thoroughly looped by the time her front doorbell rang. For a while she thought it was her ears ringing and she laughed. But the ringing continued followed by banging and yelling of her name.

She pressed her hands to her ears in an attempt to block out the offending noise that was infringing on her high.

But threats of breaking down her door filtered through the sludge in her brain. Weaving and using the furniture and wall for support she made it to the door.

Through bleary eyes she was able to make out the six bodies that stood in her doorway—maybe it was three. She braced herself against the doorframe.

"You're drunk!" the trio sang.

"And you're half-naked," Ellie added.

"Yep," Ann Marie slurred, her lopsided grin making her look even more ridiculous.

"Come inside," Barbara ordered, taking Ann Marie by the arm and ushering her into the house.

"Damn, smells like a still in here," Stephanie said, wrinkling her nose as she sniffed the air.

"Yep," Ann Marie agreed and nearly fell on the couch.

"I'm going to make some coffee," Barbara said, setting down the bag of food she carried.

"I'll get her something to put on," Ellie offered and headed to Ann Marie's bedroom.

"I'll join you for a drink if ya don't mind," Stephanie said.

"Pull up a drink...I mean a chair." Ann Marie giggled.

Stephanie sat down but didn't fix a drink. "What's going on with you, Ann?" she asked, so gently it tugged at the noose around Ann Marie's heart.

Her bottom lip trembled. She and Stephanie had been at odds for years, making a habit of rubbing each other the wrong way. But recently they'd begun to tiptoe across the divide that separated them, discovering that what set them apart were the very things that made them so much alike.

Had this been a year, even six months earlier, the last person she would have turned to in confidence would have been Stephanie.

"I feel so shaky and unsure of myself. Weak like a baby." She looked at Stephanie with such anguish in her wide eyes that Stephanie actually felt her pain.

How well Stephanie knew feelings of helplessness, to have your life and emotions controlled by forces stronger than you. It had cost her dearly over the years and she was still in the throes of relinquishing the hold her past had on her present.

"Is it Terrance?" Stephanie asked softly.

Ann Marie nodded her head and the room did a slow spin.

"Did he contact you again?"

"Yes." She swallowed. "Something I never told no one."

"What?"

"I'm still married to the bastard. Him say him coming back for me."

"Damn," Stephanie said in a hush. "What are you going to do?"

"Don't know."

"You need a good lawyer. Maybe you're not really even married anymore. It's been so long."

"I should be so lucky." She leaned back against

the couch cushions and closed her eyes just as Barbara emerged from the kitchen with a steaming cup of coffee.

"But Ann, don't you think it's time that Raquel met her father and let her make the decision for herself?"

Ann Marie jumped up so fast and the room spun so quickly she fell back down onto the couch before the words could get out of her mouth. She breathed in deeply through her nose until her stomach settled. "He'll just twist her around his finger; charm her into believing that he's the injured one."

"Is that what you're really worried about?" Barbara asked and handed her the cup of coffee.

Ann Marie took the cup in two hands and sipped the steaming black brew. "Always cut to the chase with you," she murmured.

"Everyone deserves to know them pops. True. But me t'ink once him back in Raquel's life, him be back in mine."

"What did this man do to you?" Elizabeth asked. She knew what it felt like to have a philandering husband. She'd just gotten rid of one herself. But this definitely sounded more serious that than. "Did he beat you?" she eeked out, shuddering at the thought.

She looked from one face to another. "He sexed me up so good that I haven't been right for another man since."

"Ooooh," they sang.

"We should all be so lucky," Stephanie said drolly.

"You don't know what it's like to have someone have that much control over you," Ann Marie said. "To need and want someone so badly you put up with every retched t'ing they do to keep 'em."

"Maybe he's old, bald and fat now," Stephanie offered.

"Even old, bald and fat Terrance Bishop would be more than the average woman could handle."

"Damn," they sang in harmony.

"What you need is a unified front," Barbara said and stood. She began to pace. "Once he sees that you have support, he won't try anything. You don't be alone with him. No late night dinners, no private lunches." She turned to Ann Marie and wagged a finger at her. "And don't let him in the front door. If he wants to see Raquel let them make arrangements to meet. You stay out of it. Put your foot down girl. You did it once, you can do it again."

"And get a lawyer," Stephanie said.

"For what?" Elizabeth asked.

"They're still married," Stephanie said.

Chapter 5

Terrance walked into police headquarters, dressed as usual in his tailor-made suit, shoes gleaming and his salt-and-pepper hair brushed to a soft shine, the gentle natural waves capping his perfectly shaped head. A smooth nut-brown complexion served as the canvas for jet-black almond-shaped eyes, soft curling lashes, lush lips and an alluring cleft in his solid chin.

At fifty-six he could easily pass for a man half his age. He made a point of swimming every day and would rather walk than use his many cars. The sandy beaches of Jamaica were his gym. He ran along the shore every morning for at least an hour before taking his swim in the clear blue ocean.

Now as commissioner of the police force it was more important than ever to maintain his look. It had been a long time coming. For years he'd danced in his father's shadow. But with Cyril Bishop's passing the prior year, Terrance had been appointed in his place without protest. And with position came power. With the force at his disposal and a commanding title to back him up, he'd been able to use the resources available to him to locate his wife and daughter.

His next step up the ladder was to run for office. The campaign was slated to begin in three months. His reunion with his wife and daughter would surely guarantee him the spot he coveted. A loving family always warmed a voter's heart. He intended to have his wife and daughter at his side.

"Good morning Commissioner," Stacy his latest conquest and administrative assistant greeted.

He flashed her a smile that reawakened the fire between them from the previous night. He'd have to find a way to be rid of her soon. But in the meantime she was a pleasant diversion.

"Good morning," he said in his slightly British accent, acquired from his years of education at Oxford in England.

"I left your messages on your desk."

He nodded and headed down the corridor to his office, the heavy wooden door embossed in gold letters with his name. Absently he ran his hand across the raised letters before opening the door and stepping inside.

He went to his desk and picked up the handful of messages, tossing each one aside as he reviewed them. One caught his attention.

It was from Raquel.

He came around the desk and sat down. *Call me. We need to talk.*

He licked his lips then picked up the phone, dialing the international operator. Moments later he heard the phone ringing on the other end.

"Hello?"

"Raquel. It's your dad. I just received your message."

"I wanted you to know that I've moved out of Mom's house. I'm staying in a hotel."

Terrance frowned. "Why are you in a hotel?"

"I couldn't stay there any longer."

"Did something happen? Was it because of me?"

"She lied to me all these years. She never told me about you. She never told me you were still married."

Terrance sat back in his high-backed leather chair and swiveled it to face the window.

"You shouldn't be upset with your mother." He pursed his lips, ran a finger along the thin line of his mustache.

"Why not?"

"Maybe she had her reasons." He gazed out toward the ocean, almost able to see the young Ann Marie running across the beach, her skirts held high around her thighs.

Raquel sighed into the phone. "It doesn't matter. It's done. I just wanted to leave you a number where you could reach me."

He shook the past away then took the number down.

"So, you'll stay in touch won't you?"

"Of course," he said. "Do you need money? Is there anything that I can do?"

"No. Thanks. I'm fine. You're still coming to New York aren't you?" she asked sounding like a young girl instead of a grown woman.

Terrance smiled. "Yes, darling. I'm still coming."

"Good. I'm really looking forward to meeting—seeing you."

"So am I. I'm sure you are more beautiful than I could ever imagine."

She laughed. "Mom says I look like you."

Maybe that's why it was so hard for her to love you, he thought, a constant reminder. "Well, we hope that you got the good genes." He chuckled. A knock on his door drew his attention. "I must go."

"Okay. Well, you have my number."

"Yes, and I'll be sure to call."

"Bye."

"Goodbye." He hung up the phone.

"Yes, come in."

Stacy opened the door and stepped inside. A slow smile moved across her thin mouth. She closed the door behind her and walked up to his desk. "I wanted to tell you what a nice time I had last night," she said in husky voice.

The right corner of his mouth lifted slightly. "How nice?"

She came around to his side of the desk and sat on his lap. "Why don't I show you?"

Sterling Chambers walked out of the courtroom. It had been a tough case, one that he wasn't sure he would win, but he did.

His specialty was criminal defense cases although he'd made his mark as a prosecutor. But years of putting people whom he knew to be innocent behind bars had finally taken its toll and so he'd jumped sides and opened his own practice.

It hadn't been easy, those first few years, but

he'd slowly built his business and considered himself moderately successful.

He jogged down the steps of the Supreme Court building in Manhattan and decided to take a stroll to release some of the adrenaline running through his veins. He passed by City Hall and caught a glimpse of the mayor getting into a black limo. If only he had his billions, he thought absently. The first thing he would do is revamp the school system in the inner cities. Sure it was great to have money and the power of political office, but you were always shackled by bureaucracy. And the best intentions often fell by the wayside of the political machine.

He walked along Chambers Street, sidestepping the rushing lunch-goers who were darting in and out of coffee shops and fast-food joints. He rolled his shoulders. A good massage would do wonders, he thought.

As a treat to himself he would drop by that new spa. He'd already paid for the membership, one of many, all of which he never found the time to use. But he had reason to check this one out if it would give him a chance to meet that lovely lady again. Ann Marie she said her name was. A tiny fireball. He smiled to himself.

He pulled out his cell phone from the breast pocket of his suit and turned it back on, having shut it off during the court proceedings. There were two messages from his office. None from Ann Marie.

He stuck the phone back in his pocket. He'd fix that later. Hopefully she'd be there. He was definitely looking forward to the end of the day.

When Sterling arrived at Pause it was almost six o'clock. He entered on the ground-floor level and was greeted by the scent of something absolutely delicious. His stomach growled, not having been fed since breakfast. He looked around. Several men, some in white terry robes, others in workout attire, sat around white circular wrought iron tableseating and drinking in what several nights earlier had been the reception hall.

"How may I help you?"

Sterling turned to look upon a smiling face. He recognized her from opening night also.

"I signed up during the open house and I could sure use a massage."

Elizabeth grinned. "We can make that happen. My name is Elizabeth Lewis. One of the co-owners. Why don't you come with me and we'll get you checked in. I know that Barbara—that's our masseuse—has a couple of clients ahead of you. But maybe you'd like to relax in the sauna until she's ready."

"Great." He followed her to the front desk that less than forty-eight hours ago was the bar. "You said you were a co-owner. How many owners are there? I met one the other night."

"There are four of us." She stopped at the desk and went behind it. "Which one did you meet?"

"She said her name was Ann Marie. I didn't catch her last name."

Elizabeth's eyes rolled up to meet his. "Ann Marie." She smiled. "Yep, she's one of the quartet. Actually it was Ann Marie who got us this building."

"Really?" His interest was piqued.

"She's in real estate." She opened the member file on the computer. "What's your name, sir?"

"Sterling Chambers."

She scrolled through the list of names. "Here you are." She printed out a sheet of paper and handed it to him. "When you work with Barbara give her this. She will take all your vitals and we keep it on record."

He took the paper from her hand and looked it over. "Very thorough."

"We try." She came from behind the desk. "Let me take you to a room where you can change."

"I can do that."

They both turned.

Ann Marie approached. She stuck out her hand to Sterling. "So we meet again."

He looked her over. She was just as tempting in daylight. "I was hoping that we would."

Elizabeth watched the volleyball of electricity bounce back and forth between them. *Interesting.* She hoped that Ann Marie didn't chew him up and spit him out like she did with every other man who'd crossed her path—other than Terrance.

"Since I didn't hear from you, I thought I'd force you to see me," he said in a teasing manner.

Ann Marie looked up at him. "You don't appear to be the type of man who would have to force a woman to do anything."

He grinned. "Were you planning to call?"

"At some point." She went up the stairs and he followed. "Right down this hallway is a dressing room. There are fresh robes and towels. When you're ready I'll show you to the sauna." She started to turn away.

"At what point?"

Her brow rose in question.

"At what point were you planning to call?"

"Sooner rather than later." A smile played around her mouth.

"What time do you get off?"

"Eight."

"Good. I'll be finished by then and maybe you'll join me for a late dinner."

She lifted her chin. "Are you asking me or telling me," she challenged.

"Asking, of course."

"In that case, I accept." She turned and walked away.

Sterling smiled as he watched the sway of her hips. Yeah, a little fireball.

Ann Marie returned to the front desk.

"Wow, what's going on with you two?" Elizabeth asked. "I almost got singed with the sparks."

"I barely know the man," she tossed off.

"It never stopped you before."

"Very funny."

"He seems to have a real interest in you."

"Maybe."

"Could be the one, you know."

"The one what?"

"The one to take your mind off of Terrance."

Ann Marie drew in a breath. If only, she thought. If only.

Chapter 6

Barbara and Elizabeth closed up shop while Stephanie took inventory.

"Did you work on a Sterling Chambers tonight?" Elizabeth asked innocently.

Barbara arched her aching back. "Probably, why? They're all becoming a blur at this point." She flexed her fingers. "Where's Ann Marie? I barely saw her all night."

"With that guy."

Barbara huffed. She hated it when Elizabeth grew cryptic. "What guy?" she asked, summoning her last ounce of patience.

"Sterling Chambers, silly. Who did you think I was talking about?"

Barbara flashed her a look. "Ann Marie is out with one of the clients?"

Elizabeth nodded. "Not just any client. This one is gorgeous."

"Still no excuse. We all agreed."

"Sometimes things just happen and you have to make allowances."

"I don't want this place turning into a male brothel, Ellie."

"It won't. Anyway, from what I could gather, he came on to her. Said he'd met her briefly after the opening. He seems like a really nice guy."

Barbara huffed. "She better not make a habit of that. I don't want clients getting the wrong impression about the staff."

"So do you remember him or not? Good looking, tall, athletic build, dark-skinned."

Barbara frowned in thought. "Sort of. Pull his information up." She came around the counter to stand in front of the computer.

Elizabeth typed in his name and all his information came up along with his picture that was taken when he signed up.

"Oh, yes. I remember him. Great buns and

thighs." She grinned. She looked at his information. "Ellie look, he's an attorney."

They both stared at each other as reality dawned.

"Just what Ann needs," they said in unison.

"Did you have someplace in mind?" Ann Marie
asked as they walked toward Sterling's car.

"Do you have a taste for something special?"

"I'm not choosey. But Spoonbread is really
good if you like soul food."

"I know the place, up on One-Sixteen."

"Yes."

"Spoonbread it is. My car is right over there,"
he said, pointing to the black Mercedes.

Hmm, nice.

He helped her into the car then came around to
his side. The passenger seat gently reclined when
he turned on the ignition. *Hmm, very nice.*

They drove the few blocks in an easy silence.
The local jazz station 88.3 FM played softly in the
background.

"Do you live in the area?" he asked as he
searched for a place to park.

"On Morningside. What about you?"

"Further downtown, off Central Park."

"Have you always lived in New York?"

"Actually, I grew up in Queens."

"Craziest borough I've ever been to," she scoffed. "Streets make no sense."

He chuckled. "That's a common complaint." He pulled into a space and shut off the car. The seat returned to its fully upright position.

"But you're not originally from here," he said, turning to her.

"Born in Jamaica," she said, putting her accent back in place.

He chuckled. "I've never been. I hear it's beautiful."

"It can be." She unfastened her seatbelt.

"Do I detect a note of dissatisfaction?"

"Old news, that's all."

"Maybe you'll tell me about it one day."

She kept her gaze averted. "Maybe," she said softly.

They entered the restaurant and were seated shortly thereafter.

"So I understand from one of your co-owners that you're into real estate." He looked over the menu.

"Yes. For a while now. It's a booming business especially here in the city. I'll have an iced tea," she said to the waiter who came up to their table.

"Make that two."

"Would you like to place your food order now?"

"Can you give us a few minutes?" Sterling asked.

"Sure." The waiter walked away.

"Do you have a specialty?"

"Mostly commercial properties and, over the past few years, brownstones. Those are the really hot items now."

"I've been thinking of buying, but the prices are ridiculous."

"I know. But they're beginning to come down. They have to. No one can sell properties they bought just two years ago." She paused. "Were you thinking of a brownstone or co-op?"

"Actually I'm more of a picket fence, backyard kind of guy. Guess it must be my Queens roots." He grinned and she noticed the tiny dimple in his right cheek. "And I'm not sure I want to spend my *declining* years in New York."

She laughed. "Declining. You have a long way to go, I'm sure."

"I'll be fifty in two years. It's well past time for me to begin planning out the rest of my life."

"If you're really interested I'm sure I can connect you with someone who can help with property out of state."

"I'll keep that in mind. But for now, I want to spend my pre-declining years getting to know you."

She felt her face flush. She lowered her gaze to focus on her menu. "So what kind of law do you practice?" she said, changing the subject.

"I'm a criminal defense attorney."

"That must be hard."

"It can be, especially if you lose. But now that I'm in private practice I can take on the cases that I want as opposed to the ones forced on me."

She placed her menu down and looked at him. She drew in a breath and let out what she'd been dying to know. "Can I ask you a legal question…?"

"Sure."

"When I was sixteen I was sent by my mother to live in the Bishop household. Before the year was out I was married to Terrance Bishop…"

By the time Ann Marie was done explaining her situation they were halfway through their meal. It had taken a lot for her to break her pattern of secrecy and open up to him, but she decided if there was any chance of them making it beyond tonight's dinner she was going to have to be totally honest, and either he accepted it or he didn't. All that would have been lost is some time and they both got a meal out of the deal.

Sterling put his fork down and wiped his mouth.

He was silent for a long time and Ann Marie began to grow uncomfortable. The center of his brow was a series of tight lines. Maybe it was too much too soon, she thought in retrospect.

"I'd have to do some investigating but I can certainly find out for you," he said finally. He looked across the table at her. "I know it couldn't have been easy for you to tell me all that. I appreciate your honesty."

"Are you ready to run?"

He grinned. "Tough battle is my middle name. I love a challenge. And you are certainly that, if nothing else."

She exhaled a soft sigh of relief. "So you think you can help me?"

"I can try, but only if you make me a promise."

"What kind of promise?"

"That this won't be the last time I see you and, when I do, it won't be business related."

Ann Marie bit back a grin. "I think I can help you with that."

He raised his half-empty glass of iced tea. "To more…"

She raised hers as well as her brows. "To more what?" she asked softly, leaning forward.

"To more of getting to know each other."

She touched her glass to his. "To more," she said.

* * *

When Ann Marie arrived at the spa the following afternoon it was with a new attitude. She'd had a wonderful time with Sterling. He was fun, intelligent, handsome and an absolute gentleman. What endeared him the most to her was that he was not turned off by her situation. To her that said a lot about the kind of man that he was. And maybe she was finally growing up, too. It was the first time in years that she'd actually been totally honest with a man about her past. Hopefully, it was the start of something new.

"Hey everybody," she greeted as she sauntered in, her hundred-watt smile in place.

Barbara looked over Ann Marie's shoulder. "Anybody see a weepy, fresh-mouth woman about five feet two inches tall?"

Ann Marie gave her a playful shove on the shoulder. "Oh stop. It wasn't that bad."

"Oh yes it was," Stephanie said. "Scared me." She grinned.

"Feeling better I see," Elizabeth said, walking up to join the impromptu gathering. "A handsome man wouldn't have anything to do with it would it?" She winked.

"Maybe," Ann Marie said, playing coy.

Barbara sat down on the stool by the check-in counter. "Look, Ann, I'm really glad you're feeling better. But I'm going to say this in front of everyone so that there is no misunderstanding." She drew in a breath and let it out slowly. "We need to be really careful about taking up with clients." She looked Ann Marie in the eye. "We don't want this place to get the wrong reputation."

Ann Marie cocked her hip to the side and the words flew out of her mouth so hard and fast it was difficult to understand anything other than she was pissed off. "What you saying? You t'ink me messing 'round wit the clients? That me pickin' dem up like some street walker?"

Barbara held up her palm. "Ann," she said in a tone one uses with an excitable child. "That's not what I'm saying."

"Well what are ya saying then?"

"Be careful and mindful that's all."

"Listen hon," Elizabeth said, "We're happy if you're happy." She turned her gaze on Barbara. "You didn't meet him here anyway. Not exactly. So it's not the same thing."

Ann Marie huffed and folded her arms.

"That's all I'm saying," Barbara added. She stepped up to Ann Marie and put her arm around her tense shoulders. "I hear he's a lawyer."

Ann Marie looked up at her. "How did you know that?"

"We looked him up?" Elizabeth beamed.

"Maybe he could help you with your Terrance problem," Stephanie said.

"You all have this figured out, huh?"

"We thought it would be a good idea. I mean you can always ask him hypothetically, 'cause we know how you are about your personal life," Barbara said.

"Well for your information, me did tell him. Told him everything."

"You did?" they echoed in disbelief. First the tears and then true confessions. What next?

Ann Marie nodded.

Barbara had to sit down. "Well, what did he say?"

"Him say he loves a challenge. And…he wants to see me again." Her smile lit up the room.

"Truth is good for the soul," Elizabeth said preaching to the choir.

Ann Marie took a seat next to Barbara. "It was scary, you know." She looked from one face to the next. "It's easy to keep folks at a distance, not let them get too close." She lowered her gaze and focused on her Jimmy Choos. "Been that way all my life." She drew in a breath then looked up. "But something hit me last night. I realized that all the secrets, all the keeping folks at bay had hurt me more than helped. And me tired of hurting all the time," she added in a whisper.

"It's gonna be fine, girl," Stephanie said. "Just wait and see."

"Yeah," Elizabeth agreed. "Just wait and see."

Barbara uh-huhed her response but silently wondered just how fine it would all turn out.

Chapter 7

Wil Hutchinson pulled himself up the steps to his third floor walk-up apartment favoring his left hip. It had been a long day. His mail delivery route took him up and down the rolling hills of upper Manhattan. He sure wasn't as young and spry as he used to be, he thought ruefully to himself. He'd been a mail carrier for almost thirty years and had watched Harlem change from an oasis for black culture replete with supper clubs, soul-food restaurants, men who sported real hats and women who wore gloves on Sundays—to high-end department stores, super food chains instead of the mom and pop corner store and a steady influx of wealthy white yuppies who saw gold in the historic brownstones.

That was then, he mused, turning his key in the lock. Time changes everything, especially the body. He passed his reflection in the hallway mirror and immediately sucked in his stomach and straightened his back.

He wasn't a bad looking man. Most women thought him to be handsome. But he'd put on the pounds and, years without a real woman to please, he'd let himself go. His days consisted of work and his evenings of keeping an eye on his teenaged son, Chauncey. Wil had big plans for his son. Next year he would be in college. He'd saved most of his life to ensure that he'd had the funds available to pay for Chauncey's education. But he'd also taught his son about the value of hard work and that making one's way in the world was how he would get to be a real man.

Wil set down his backpack on the kitchen table and looked up at the clock above the fridge. His son should be walking through the door any minute from his job at the Schomburg. He'd been working at the historic library since he was old enough to get working papers. The pay wasn't great but it helped and Wil made sure that Chauncey saved more than he spent.

He was just about to get an iced cold beer when he heard the front door open.

"Dad, you home?" Chauncey yelled out.

Wil shook his head and laughed. They'd been roommates for the past ten years since his mother walked out on them and never a day passed that Chauncey didn't yell the same question. It was almost as if he was afraid that one day he'd come home and his dad would be gone, too.

"In here, son."

Chauncey came bounding in the kitchen, all six-foot-two-inches of him. Every time Wil looked at his son he was amazed that he'd been part of creating such a good looking boy. Chauncey had never been plagued with adolescent acne. His skin was still smooth and clear with red undertones highlighting his bronze complexion, a throwback to his American Indian ancestry. But it was his eyes that captured the attention of everyone who met him, they were a light brown, the color of sweet tea and when the mood hit them, they turned a deep green.

"How was your day?" Wil asked, taking the beer and twisting of the top. He'd taken two long swallows before Chauncey could respond.

"Pretty cool." He plopped down in a wooden chair at the decades old butcher-block table. "Hey, Dad…"

"Hmm?" Wil closed the fridge and opened the

freezer, searching for something to get started for dinner.

"You know how you've been saying as soon as you get some time you were going to go to the gym?"

"Yeah," he replied absently, pushing aside frozen packages of vegetables.

"Well, I signed you up."

Wil stopped his search and turned, a frown tightening his features. "Say what?"

Chauncey grinned. "I signed you up."

"Signed me up where, boy?"

He pulled a brochure from his back pocket and handed it to his father.

"Pause for Men? What the hell is that?"

Chauncey chuckled. "It's a day spa, just for men. They have exercise, massage, steam room, the works. And they serve health food," he added.

"This must cost a fortune. We can't afford something like this. I can go to the Y."

"Dad, your year membership is all paid for."

"What?" His eyes widened.

"I took care of it." Chauncey stood. "Out of money I've been saving."

"That's for school. We discussed that."

"I'll be fine. I wanted to do this for you. You've been taking care of me. Let me do something for you."

"Chauncey…"

"It's a done deal. And you know how you are about wasting money. So you know you're going to have to go."

Wil heaved a breath. "Maybe you can still get your money back."

"I don't want to. As a matter of fact, I thought I'd walk with you over there…tonight."

"Tonight!"

Chauncey laughed. "Yeah, tonight. So why don't you get showered, put on something comfortable and we can head out in about an hour. You always told me why put off until tomorrow what you can do today."

"Don't you have homework?"

"No excuses."

"What about dinner?"

"You can eat there and I'll fix myself something."

Wil slowly saw himself losing the battle. Chauncey could be just about as difficult and stubborn as him. He glanced down at the brochure again. He opened it and looked at the high-gloss pictures of the interior. What the hell? He couldn't disappoint his son and he certainly wasn't going to waste any money. Maybe it would all work out. Might not be so bad, he thought, walking slowly to his bedroom as he read the material. Might not be so bad at all.

Barbara applied massage oil to the back of her latest client. He sighed in pleasure as her strong fingers kneaded the tight muscles of his back.

"That feels wonderful," he moaned.

Barbara smiled. "You have a lot of knots in your back. Comes from tension. You should be sure to get a massage at least once per week until I can get them all out."

"If it feels anything like this, you won't have a problem out of me." He chuckled.

"Okay, all done." She turned her back as he sat up. "Thanks."

She made some notes in his file then turned to face him. "You can take this to the front desk on your way out and someone will put it in the computer. You can schedule your next session at the same time." She smiled and handed him the card.

"Sure thing, thanks again." He walked out.

Barbara drew in a long breath. She was exhausted. She looked up on the schedule she had posted on the wall. She had a half-hour break before her next client. Relieved, she sat down. What she really wanted to do was stretch out on the massage table and take a quick power nap.

Since her conversation with Michael she hadn't really slept well. She yawned.

If only Michael could see that what she did here at the spa had no sexual undertones at all. She was strictly professional and her posture commanded that she be treated that way from her clients.

His whole attitude was troubling. But what was even more disturbing was his notion that she was going to give up everything and go off to la la land to live happily ever after with nothing to do all day besides shop and be his wife.

She frowned. There was so much more to her than that. She'd worked all her life and was proud of her accomplishments. With her experience and certifications she could work anywhere in the country. Some women may dream of the day when they did nothing more than watch the soaps and go to luncheons. But she wasn't one of them.

A soft knock on the door interrupted her musings. "Yes?"

Elizabeth poked her head in. "All clear?"

"Sure. Come on in."

"I know this is your break time, but we have a new client who came in. I've given him the grand tour but I was hoping you could tell him about what you do."

Barbara stretched. "Okay, I'll be right out."

"Thanks. I'll let him know."

There goes my break, she thought, taking off her smock and hanging it on the back of the door. She hand brushed her hair into her ponytail and went out to meet their new client.

When Barbara approached the front desk, she stopped short and so did her heart. It couldn't be, she thought. She blinked several times thinking that maybe she was seeing things. But when her vision cleared, it wasn't an illusion. *Still unmistakable*.

She swallowed over the sudden dryness in her throat and nearly choked. Before anyone spotted her she darted down the hall to the staff kitchen and took a bottle of water from the fridge. After several gulps her head cleared. Steeling herself, she walked out of the kitchen to face her past.

Chapter 8

Stephanie left the spa earlier than usual. She felt bad leaving them short handed, but she had no choice. St. Ann's, the rehabilitation center that housed her twin sister Samantha, had called saying that Sam was having a really bad day and perhaps it would help if she saw her.

She'd been negligent she knew. With the opening of the spa and all the work leading up to it, she hadn't been to see her sister as regularly as she generally did. And now that Tony was in her life, it was one more thing to take her mind away from her obligation to her sister.

She pulled up in front of the center and drove into the lot. Moments later she was walking through the door. It was dinnertime and the hallways were busy with the nurses and the aides delivering meals to those who were unable to come to the community cafeteria and ambulatory patients who were slowly making their way to dinner.

Stephanie stopped at the front desk. "Hi, I got here as quickly as I could," she said to the nurse.

"Oh, Ms. Moore." The nurse smiled at Stephanie. "Your sister will be so glad to see you."

"The caller said she was having a bad day," Stephanie asked more than stated.

"I'm sure her doctor can fill you in on all the details. He's actually in with her now."

"Thanks." Stephanie adjusted her purse on her shoulder and walked down the corridor toward her sister's room. When she reached the door she could hear the doctor's voice talking gently to Samantha.

For a moment, Stephanie squeezed her eyes shut and drew in a breath of strength. She was almost afraid to go in but knew that she must.

She turned the knob on the door and walked in.

The doctor turned upon her approach. Slowly he stood up, keeping a comforting hand on Samantha's shoulder. Stephanie could see that she'd been crying. Her heart ached.

She came fully into the room, putting her purse on the bed as she approached Sam. She knelt down in front of her and stroked her cheek.

"Sweetie, it's me Stephanie."

Samantha's bottom lip trembled as if she were going to cry again.

"It's okay. I'm here now," she said softly then looked up at Dr. Nelson.

He gave a subtle toss of his head toward the door.

Slowly Stephanie rose. "I'll be right back. I'm going to talk to Dr. Nelson for a minute."

They stepped outside and closed the door.

"What's going on? What happened?"

Dr. Nelson folded his hands in front of him. "She had a major episode today. She's been crying almost constantly and that's not like Sam. She refuses to eat and…she's been trying to talk."

"Talk!" Stephanie's mind raced. Sam hadn't uttered a word in nearly two decades. Not since the night of the accident. She barely seemed to pay attention to the world around her except for brief flashes. "Are you sure? What did she say?"

"We're pretty sure she called your name. At least she tried to. And she became very agitated."

Stephanie's hand flew to her chest. "My God. I…"

"We were just as surprised. Tomorrow we

want to run some tests, a CAT and a PET scan to reevaluate brain function. Something is obviously going on."

"But all the doctors said she'd never get better."

"I'm not saying that she will either. But something is happening. We need to know what it is."

Stephanie slowly nodded her head, trying to take it all in. "And you'll let me know?"

"Of course."

"So…what if there is new activity, then what?"

"If, and I say *if,* that is the case then we would put her on a new rehab regime that would include speech therapy, something she's showed no need of since she's been here."

She didn't want to hope. She'd given up hoping a long time ago.

"There is one thing, however."

Stephanie returned her focus on the doctor. "What's that?"

"If in fact there is some indication that her speech is returning, she's going to need a lot of work."

"Which means more money," she translated.

"I'm afraid so. At the present time your monthly bill only takes care of room and board and basic services. If we begin to incorporate speech therapy into her daily routine…" He let the rest hang in the air.

"How much are we talking about?"

"Let's cross that bridge when we come to it. It may or may not be necessary but I wanted you to be aware of the possibility."

"Sure."

"I'll let you get to your visit. If you have any questions before you leave have the nurse page me."

"Thank you, Doctor."

He nodded and walked away.

Stephanie stood on the outside of Samantha's door. *More money?* Since she'd left her job at the PR firm, she'd been using her savings to cover the cost of Samantha's care. Her private business had yet to take off fully and it was too soon for the spa to show any profits. She had no clue how she was going to be able to pull any more green rabbits out of the hat.

Sighing, she put on her best face and went in to be with her sister.

He sensed her the way you can feel an impending rain shower after a long drought; from the ache that settles deep in your bones to the parched dryness in the back of your throat. You long for the rain to replenish you, wash away the misery of living without it. But at the same time are aware that it has the power to drown you.

Slowly he turned around. For an instant time moved backward. They were young and in love with the whole world ahead of them. Barbara and Wil against the world. That's what they'd said, but it wasn't what they'd meant. At least that's not how it turned out.

Recognition, memories danced in the reflection of their eyes. Then like the final curtain, their eyes shuttered the past and it was gone.

Barbara gripped the water bottle in one hand, her mouth in a tight line, and forced one foot in front of the other.

"There you are," Elizabeth chirped. She extended her hand toward Wil and his son then Barbara, unfazed by the tension that bounced between them like a rapidly fired tennis ball. "This is Mr. Hutchinson and his son, Chauncey."

His son. My God. Her knees felt weak.

"This is Barbara Allen, our resident specialist." She smiled at Barbara but it faded like bleach splashed on color. She turned halfway to Barbara. "Are you all right?" she asked under her breath.

"Yes. Fine. You can go cover the front." She forced a smile.

Elizabeth's gaze darted back and forth between the two, ready to jump in and defend her friend if need be, before she finally walked away.

"Well," Barbara said on a breath, "we can't have our new clients standing around. I'll take you over to the sauna room and then the massage rooms."

"Sounds great."

It was the first time she'd heard the low rumble of his voice in almost thirty years and it still had the power to send shivers running through her belly.

Lawd don't let me faint and make a fool of myself.

"Would your son like to come as well?" she asked, focusing on the top button of Wil's shirt instead of his eyes.

"Naw, I'm cool. You go ahead, Dad. I'm gonna hang out at the café."

"I'll meet you there when I'm done." He turned his attention back to Barbara. "Lead the way."

Barbara bit down on her bottom lip then headed toward the basement. She could feel the heat of his body behind her.

"We, uh, had to put the sauna down here because of all the water and the heat factor," she rambled. "But it doesn't look anything like a basement." She laughed nervously.

"How long are we going to pretend that we don't know each other?"

The question grabbed her by the arm and tugged, but she didn't slow her step.

"I thought maybe that's the way you wanted it." She kept walking passed the sauna stalls.

Steam seeped from beneath the doors giving the illusion that they were walking on clouds or in some kind of MTV video, making the entire encounter even more surreal.

"We have eight enclosed saunas and a steam room," she said in a practiced tour guide voice.

"Barbara." This time it was Wil's hand that grabbed her. "Wait. Look at me." She stood still. "Please."

With great reluctance she turned around. Her eyes started at his feet, timidly making their way up the length of his body—taking him all in—remembering. They rose until they rested on his face—the one she vowed to forget but hadn't.

"You're still as pretty as I remember." His dark eyes traveled leisurely across her face, down the slope of her neck.

Barbara was never happier than at that moment, pleased with the fact that she could actually stand there and not have to hold her breath and her stomach in until he looked away.

"So you have a son," she said in a voice that sounded as if it came from far away.

"Yes."

"Good looking young man."

"I'd tell him but he's already vain."

He smiled and she swore she heard a symphony. "He got it honest," she admitted.

Wil had barely changed in the years since way back when, she observed. He still had that incredible cocoa-brown skin, broad shoulders that could always carry the weight of her world. Eyes so soft and brown you wanted them all over you. She remembered those lips, the way they used to nibble on her ear or plant hot kisses on her young neck. He'd gained some weight. They all had. There were dashes of gray in his close cut hair and mustache, but it only made him seem more virile, more…man.

A hot shot of desire exploded right between her legs sending a tremor along the inside of her thighs. *Ohmygoodness.*

"How long have you been working here?" he asked, snapping her out of her trance.

She blinked. "Uh, I'm one of the co-owners, actually."

"Really."

Genuine surprise lit his eyes and admiration tugged up the corners of his mouth.

He slid his hands into the pocket of his sweatpants. She thought about her diamond, thankful that she'd taken it off to work. A little stab of guilt wiggled under her skin. *Glad she'd taken it off? Why?*

"How many co-owners are there?"

"Huh?"

He repeated the question.

"Oh, sorry. There are four of us. You met Ellie and then there's Ann Marie and Stephanie."

He chuckled, his eyes sparkling with merriment. "Four women open a spa for men. That's rich." He chuckled harder.

Barbara put her hand on her hip and tilted her head to the side. "I really don't see what's so funny."

"Not that it's funny, ha ha funny. But funny in the brilliant sense. Pure genius." He stopped chuckling and looked dead at her. "Who knows what men want more than a woman?"

Her breath stopped somewhere in her chest and refused to move. She started to feel lightheaded and began coughing—choking was more like it.

Alarmed, Wil sprung into action and began patting her back. "Are you all right? Can I get you something?"

She bent over, still coughing, but loving the feel of those big hands on her back, the sound of his voice in her ear. She unscrewed the cap on her bottle of water and took a long swallow.

By degrees her coughing subsided and she

slowly stood up. "Sorry about that," she choked out. "Guess something went down the wrong way."

"Sure you're okay?"

She nodded.

"Married?" he asked out of the blue.

She almost lapsed into another coughing attack. "No. Widowed."

"Sorry."

She dared to look at him. "You?"

"Was. It's been over for years now."

"So you're a single parent."

"That's what they call us." He waited a beat. "Kids?"

"No," she barely murmured.

He lowered his gaze for an instant, not wanting to witness the sadness he saw in hers. "Sorry."

"It's okay. I've gotten over that part of my life." She drew in a breath. "Well, if we don't finish this tour your son will be wondering what I've done with you down here."

"I could think of a few things, but then there might be witnesses."

She didn't even want to begin to imagine what he meant by that. "Uh, down this hallway is the massage room." She caught his grin before she turned away.

"So you do the massages?" he asked looking around.

"Yes, but we're in the process of hiring some permanent help. My full-time job is at the hospital in rehabilitation. I'm on vacation this week."

"Wow. I'm impressed." He frowned for a moment, trying to put it together in his head. "So you only do this part-time. How long have you been open?"

She grinned. "This is only day two if you can believe it."

He chuckled. "Now I really am impressed. Like I said, pure genius. You ladies have a goldmine here."

"We hope so."

"So what does a hardworking brother need to do to sign up for a well-deserved massage?"

"Uh, it can be taken care of at the front desk."

His gaze held her in place.

"You look good woman."

The pulse in her throat went on a rampage. "Thank you," she managed to say.

She watched his shoulders rise and fall.

"Guess I better get back."

She nodded numbly.

They stood staring at each other for what felt like a wonderful eternity.

Finally, Wil said, "After you."

Barbara shook off the cobwebs forming around her brain and led the way back to the front desk.

Elizabeth was working with a client.

"Uh, I can get you all signed up or you can wait for Elizabeth."

"If you're not busy…"

She thought about her next client that was due any minute. But she also wanted just a few more minutes alone with Wil.

"Sure. Have a seat." She walked behind the check-in counter. "I just need to get some information from you…"

As she listened to him respond to her questions, his answers hit her like tiny pellets. Marital Status: Divorced; Next of Kin: Son; D.O.B.: September 20, 1952; Contact #: 212 555-8855; Height: 6'3", Weight: 225 lbs.; Employer: USPS; Mailing Address: One Hundred and Thirty-Eighth Street; Method of Payment: Fully paid—cash.

She now knew where he lived and worked— right in her own backyard—for years. They didn't call New York City the melting pot for no reason. You could come here and virtually disappear in the stew. She had his home number. But she wouldn't use it. It was against policy. The very same policy she'd admonished Ann Marie about.

She hit the Save button then asked him to face the Webcam and she took his picture for the files.

"Well, all done." She handed him his membership card.

"Can I make that appointment now?" He leaned casually against the counter.

Her eyes darted around for a minute. "Uh, sure." She cleared her throat. "Do you have a day in mind?"

"How about tomorrow around seven?"

She swallowed as she brought up the schedule on the screen. "I'm booked at seven but I have an opening at six."

"Fine. Six." He stood back. "I'll see you then."

Before she could respond in the slightest, he turned and walked toward the café.

Barbara was shaking all over. Not in a lifetime did she think she'd see him again. And here of all places. She'd never told Marvin about Wil. She'd never told the girls, either.

But life being what it was, the long buried secret of her past would be all over the place in a heartbeat.

Chapter 9

Sterling twirled the pen around between his fingers, ruminating over the information he'd gathered regarding Ann Marie and her marriage.

He tossed the pen aside and watched it roll across the desk until it ran into a crystal paperweight of the scales of justice and stopped.

The U.S. laws and those of Jamaica were a bit different on this particular issue. He'd hoped to have found a loophole of some sort, but that was not the case.

He hadn't bargained on getting involved with a married woman. If he really wanted to be honest with himself, he had no real desire for any long lasting commitment in any form. Marriage was not in the cards for him. He enjoyed the life of a bachelor and couldn't imagine coming home to the same face day after day.

He swung his chair toward the window and looked out upon the Manhattan skyline. Ann Marie caught his eye. No question. There was something about her that was no-nonsense and vulnerable at the same time—a lethal combination. He could only imagine all that island fire let loose.

He drew in a breath, turned his chair back toward his desk and dialed the cell phone number she'd given him.

Ann Marie had finished up with her last real estate client of the morning and was preparing to leave and head over to the spa when her cell phone rang. She checked the number on the lighted dial. A slow smile eased across her lips.

"Hi."

"Hey there. Did I catch you at a bad time?"

"No, not at all. I was just leaving to head over to the spa."

"I have some free time. What if I meet you over there?"

Barbara's warning sounded in her head. She

ignored it. "Sure. I should be there in about a half hour. I'll meet you in the café. Don't know what's on the menu, but I'm sure it's something good."

"Perfect. I have about two hours then I need to get back for court."

"See you then." She disconnected the call and dropped the phone in her purse. "I'm gone for the rest of the day," she called out.

Carol popped up from behind her desk just as Ann Marie passed by.

"Ann Marie." She looked around as if she expected something awful to happen to her.

Ann Marie stood and tried to keep the annoyance off her face and out of her voice.

"Yes?"

Carol came from behind her desk. She kept her voice low. "A call came in for you earlier. You were with a client."

Ann Marie frowned. "So why didn't you just give it to me?" she snapped.

"I just thought…well, I've been watching you lately and you haven't been yourself since those flowers came."

Now she really was annoyed and not afraid to show it. "What does that have to do with giving me my messages? That's your job!"

Carol was unfazed by Ann Marie's growing ire.

"The message was from the same man who sent the flowers...and called the other day. It seemed to upset you so much. So I didn't say anything because I didn't want to see you upset again."

The plaintive tone reached that hidden spot in Ann Marie's heart. She felt herself soften to this silly girl who maybe wasn't so silly after all, but simply a nice girl who cared.

Ann Marie lowered her head. She had to stop thinking the worst of everyone. She finally looked at Carol.

"I...appreciate your concern. But I can handle my business." She paused, taking in the sunken expression on Carol's face. "Thank you. Very much."

A smile sprung across Carol's mouth. "No problem. Any way I can help." She started to return to her desk.

"Uh, Carol..."

"Yes?" She frowned for a moment.

"The message..."

"Oh." She sputtered a nervous laugh. She plucked the message slip from her desk and gingerly handed it to Ann Marie.

Ann Marie stared down at the neat script. *Terrance Bishop. Please return the call. Important.*

Tightness built in her chest. What could Terrance possibly want now? Hadn't he just about ruined everything already? And they hadn't even seen each other yet. She looked around. The office was buzzing with activity. She shoved the note in her purse. She'd call him from her cell phone once she got in her car.

She pushed through the glass and wood door and stepped out into the steamy afternoon. August had been barely tolerable and September still had a hold on them. She loosened the top button of her blouse then deactivated the alarm on her car.

Slipping inside she immediately turned on the engine followed by the air conditioning. She sat there for a few minutes until the car began to cool. She stole a glance at her purse almost as if the note inside was calling out to her, whispering her name—in Terrance's voice.

She shook off the sensation. The hell with Terrance Bishop. Whatever he wanted would wait. She'd promised to meet Sterling and she had no intention of keeping him waiting.

When she pulled up across the street from Pause she caught a glimpse of Sterling walking inside. Her heart thumped one good time. He sure was a good looking man, she mused, watching the way his body fit just right in his pinstriped suit and the easy way he moved. She sat there staring until he disappeared inside and a car horn blared behind her to get out of the way. She glanced over her shoulder, wanted to give the impatient driver the finger but changed her mind. The last thing she needed was an incident in front of her place of business. She pulled off and cruised around the block several times before she found a parking space.

By the time she got inside she'd already lost fifteen precious minutes.

"Hey Ann," Elizabeth greeted from the front desk. "Glad you're here. I desperately need to take a break. Barbara is busy with a client and Stephanie is holding it down in the exercise room." She shook her head and stepped from behind the desk. "We have got to get some more help in here and quick. Desiree is in the café. She and Dawne are taking turns but they have their own business to run."

Elizabeth rambled on about the staffing shortage and all Ann Marie wanted to do was make a quick dash in Sterling's direction. From her vantage point she could see him in the café area.

"I saw Mr. Chambers a minute ago. But he didn't look like he was here for any treatment. He didn't even sign in, even though I asked him to." She sounded annoyed. "He went straight to the café."

"I know, I was supposed to meet him here for a quick lunch. He has to get back to court this afternoon."

"Well maybe you can explain the policy. Every member needs to check in when they arrive. We need to know exactly who is here, when and for how long. Know what I mean? We're liable for everyone who sets foot in the door."

Ann Marie twisted her lips in annoyance. Since when had the not-too-long-ago Suzy Homemaker become such a stickler for business rules and etiquette? It was right on Ann Marie's tongue to say as much, but she'd made a mini-promise to herself not to think so badly of other people. The flipside was Elizabeth was right. The last thing they needed was someone claiming something happened to them on the premises and they weren't even there.

"I'll be sure to remind him. He was probably in a hurry."

Elizabeth huffed. "Thanks. I'll be back in about fifteen minutes." She started to walk away.

"Ellie."

She turned, her usual amicable demeanor back in place.

"Do me a quick favor. Drop in the café and just let Sterling know that I'm tied up for a few minutes."

"Sure." She walked toward the café while Ann Marie took her spot behind the desk.

Folks sure were changing, Ann Marie thought as she sat down. There was a time when Elizabeth would have put her own needs aside and let Ann Marie go to Sterling, nor would she have had the backbone to give her a lecture on business. Go figure. Maybe her impending divorce from Matt was finally putting some starch in her spine.

She stuck her purse in the desk drawer just as Sterling walked up.

"Hey," he said.

She smiled. "Hey yourself. Sorry about the delay. First it was parking, now it's staffing."

"Not a problem. I totally understand." He checked his watch. "Unfortunately, I don't have as much time as I thought I would. Traffic was brutal getting here from downtown. I don't want to get stuck going back and be late for court."

"Sure." She looked around quickly. "We can talk here."

He leaned against the counter. "I'll get right to the point. According to everything I've found out, you are still very much married to Terrance Bishop. It doesn't matter that it's been so many years since you two have lived together or even communicated. I was hoping to find some kind of loophole but there aren't any."

Her spirits sank.

"Cheer up," he said, reading the look in her eyes. "Maybe that's why he wants to see you, to finally put an end to it all. Maybe he wants to get married again."

Something sharp stuck her in the center of her chest. An image of her wedding day on the balmy island of Jamaica leaped into her mind. They'd gotten married on the beach with the midnight blue sky and the stars as their canopy. Coconut and palm trees danced with the ocean breeze. She was young, in love and walking down an aisle made of tropical flowers toward the man that was to be her husband and father of her child. She thought it would be forever, that her love would tame his wild ways.

Terrance married again—to someone else? The idea had never occurred to her. As much as she'd distanced herself from her husband and her marriage, she'd never envisioned Terrance with someone else—at least not a wife.

"Are you okay?"

She blinked then focused on Sterling. She flashed a half-hearted smile. "Fine. Taking it in I guess." She drew in a breath. "Nothing in this life is easy."

Sterling chuckled. "That's an understatement." He waited a beat. "Listen I have to run. Sorry I couldn't have been a bearer of better news. But as a consolation, I'd love to take you out tonight."

Her expression brightened. "I'd really like that."

"What time do you get off?"

"We close at nine. Is that too late?"

"We'll both be good and starved by then. I have an idea—if you're willing to take chances."

She frowned. "What kind of chances?"

"I should be finished in court by five. I'll dart to the market, fix dinner and then pick you up. We can eat at my place, relax, talk and unwind. How's that sound?"

Her features creased. "Can you cook?"

Sterling laughed from deep in his stomach. "I haven't killed anyone yet."

"That's not very comforting." She eyed him for a moment. "On one condition."

"What's that?"

She wagged her finger at him. "Don't be late."

He grinned. "Nine on the dot." He took her finger, leaned over and kissed her softly on the lips, taking her by complete surprise. He paused inches away from her mouth. "Hope that's not against the rules," he whispered.

If it was she didn't care. "I'll have to look that up in the employee handbook," she said.

He grinned. "See you at nine."

"Oh, wait. Why don't I just come directly to your place? I want to go home and change first. Is that okay?"

"Sure." He gave her the address. "So then I'll see you around ten. Is an hour enough time?"

"Sure." She smiled.

"Great. See you later."

She watched him leave and began counting the hours, Terrance all but forgotten.

Chapter 10

Stephanie tried to keep her attention focused on the client who was asking about lifetime membership. She rattled off something that sounded relatively intelligent but her mind was on her own dilemma—getting enough money to facilitate the additional care her sister would need. Her visit to the facility earlier had left her more shaken than she'd let on.

She smiled her best PR smile as the client left, hopefully satisfied with whatever it was she'd told him.

With a few moments of downtime she returned

to the office. They'd sent out information on the
positions available and she wanted to check her
e-mail and phone messages for any responses.

She opened the e-mail file on the computer and
was very pleased with what she saw. Just a quick
glance showed that there were more than twenty
responses from *Craig's List* as well as the Swedish
Institute that trained massage therapists. They'd
used two of the students on opening night. They'd
done an excellent job. Stephanie tucked their information in a folder.

She opened each e-mail and noted the qualifications, printing out those that met the require-
ments. By the time she was done, she had a solid
fifteen candidates to choose from. She stuck the
resumes in the folder and marked it Applicants.
When Pause closed for the night, she and the girls
would have to go over them and start setting up
interviews as soon as possible.

With that task aside she was forced to revisit her
circumstances. Although Dr. Nelson didn't say
how much more it would cost, she had a feeling it
would be substantial.

A giddy feeling bubbled around in her stomach.
Samantha talking again. She slowly shook her
head. The doctors over the years had given her no
hope that it was possible. She'd eventually re-

signed herself to the idea that Samantha would never come back to her.

She sighed and leaned back in the chair. They'd had such a short time together and it was all her fault. If she hadn't insisted that Samantha accompany her to that party… She let the thought end there. She'd whipped herself with the lash of guilt for years, it colored everything that she did right up to getting involved with Conrad—her ex, very married boss. That was still an unresolved issue. Yeah, she'd quit, leaving him and the company high and dry, but it hadn't stopped his wife from contacting her.

She was still getting anonymous calls to her home, hang ups in the middle of the night. She knew it was that crazy woman—even though her caller ID always read Unknown Caller. Other than being an obnoxious irritant, Stephanie wasn't sure what the missus hoped to gain besides depriving her of a decent night's sleep.

It was beginning to affect her relationship with Tony to a point where she didn't want to risk him spending the night at her house, or any long period of time for that matter. He wanted to know why and she didn't want to tell him, so she came up with various excuses: the apartment is being painted, fumigated, no food in the fridge, noisy neighbors, air conditioning not working, she hadn't cleaned. At some point he was going to think she had someone living with her. When she went by his place, she'd stayed over a couple of times and although they hadn't slept together, it was definitely heading in that direction.

The phone rang, jarring her from her troubling thoughts.

"Good afternoon, Pause for Men, Stephanie speaking."

"Hey sweetie, glad I got you."

His spidey sense must really be working, Stephanie thought mildly amused. "How are you?"

"Busy day. I've been running all over town tying up some loose ends with two new clients."

"Two! Wow. That's great."

"Yeah, one wants me to design a corporate website and the other needs a complete promotional package."

"Congratulations. That's great news."

"That's what I thought. I wanted to celebrate."

"Sounds great. What did you have in mind?"

"Well, I have tickets to see *The Color Purple,* for tomorrow night. Can you get off by six?"

"I'm sure I can work it out." She'd have to come up with some story to tell the girls. The fact that she was going out on a date when they were so shorthanded would not sit well.

"Great. Then I figured we'd have dinner and then I'd come over to your place since I have an early appointment the following day in your area."

She gulped. *Her place.* "Oh—"

"And I don't care about paint, things that go bump in the night, rap music or an echo in your fridge."

She almost laughed but it wasn't funny. How was she going to get around it this time?

"So…how 'bout it? I can do the couch thing if that's what you're worried about. Like I told you, I care about you and I'm a patient man. You don't have to worry about me slipping between your sheets unless you invite me."

Damn, who could say no to all that? She'd just disconnect the phone and hope that no emergency arose during the night.

"I think it's a great idea."

"Perfect. So should I pick you up at the job?"

Ouch, the other dilemma. "Hmm, I think I'll dart home to change. You can pick me up there by six."

"Works for me. I'll see you tomorrow."

"Okay. Bye."

"Bye, babe, I'll call you tonight." He hung up.

Stephanie held the phone in her hand until the dial tone hummed in her ear. What would life be without one obstacle after another, she thought. *Easy, that's what.*

Resigned to her present situation, she signed off from the e-mail, pushed away from the desk and headed back out front; praying that the rest of the day would go by without a hitch.

When she came up front she gasped out loud. Standing at the check-in desk chatting it up with Elizabeth was Conrad Hendricks.

Why didn't New York City have earthquakes, because she sure wished the earth would open and swallow him whole.

Straightening her shoulders and steeling her expression she marched over to the desk.

"I'll take care of this," she said to Elizabeth with such an edge to her voice, Elizabeth jerked back.

Stephanie flashed on Conrad. "We're at capacity in terms of membership," she said. She folded her arms.

Conrad put on the charm. His light gray eyes darkened as he took her in.

"It's been awhile," he said softly.

Stephanie lifted her chin and began moving away from the desk out of Elizabeth's range of hearing, forcing Conrad to move with her.

"What do you want?" she said from between clenched teeth.

He looked around, a smile as big as Madison

Square Garden on his face. "The place has been all over the news and in the Style section of the papers." He focused those gray clouds on her. "I saw your signature style all over the news blitz." He stepped closer. She stepped back. "So I thought I'd come over and see for myself."

"You've seen, now you can leave."

"But I've only just arrived. I'd really like it if you showed me around." He took her arm.

She stole a look around her, dragged in a breath. "Take your hand off of me," she hissed.

"Still feisty. But that's what I always loved about you."

Her head began to pound.

"I want to see you, Stephanie. I miss you."

"You have a wife who seems to enjoy calling my home at all hours of the night. Go home."

"Marilyn's been calling you?"

He actually looked surprised, which caught her off guard.

"Don't act like you don't know," she said, without much force.

"I didn't know."

"According to your wife she got the number from you and you told her I'd practically been stalking you and wouldn't let you end the relationship."

He shook his head sharply. "I haven't said

anything to her." He frowned, his gaze drifted away for a moment then settled back on her.

"You really don't know do you?"

"That's what I'm telling you. Whatever Marilyn did she did on her own."

"Then you really do need to go home and talk to your wife. For all you know she could be having you followed and I damn sure don't want her showing up here."

His jaw flexed. "I'll take care of Marilyn."

"Good." She started to move away.

"Stephanie."

"What is it?" she asked as she turned back toward him.

"I meant what I said. I want to see you. I miss you."

"Forget it Conrad. It's over. There's nothing left to talk about."

"Even if I told you I was leaving Marilyn."

She flinched. Words she never thought she'd hear him say. The mistress never gets the husband. Statistics were against her.

She lifted her chin. "Good. I hope you made the right decision. I have to get back to work." She walked away and kept going right past the check-in desk and Elizabeth, who was trying to get her attention and talk on the phone at the same time.

Stephanie went back to the office and quickly shut the door behind her.

Conrad showing up here! What next? She paced back and forth in front of the square metal desk, chewing on her recently manicured thumbnail. Leaving his wife? How did she feel about that? Did it even matter?

The office door opened and Elizabeth came in. "Who was that? Are you all right?" She came in and closed the door.

"Yeah. I'm fine. Really." She glanced away then sat down on the edge of the desk.

"So...who was that?"

"Conrad."

She frowned for a moment in thought. Then her eyes widened in realization. "*The* Conrad?"

"One and the same."

"What did he want?"

She snorted out a laugh. "To tell me he's leaving his wife."

Elizabeth sat down. "And?"

"And he wants to see me."

"You're not going to do it are you?"

She hadn't told anyone about what happened that last time with Conrad or how over the months leading toward their burning conclusion how rough and abusive he'd become. That had been her dirty little secret. The fact that she'd confessed to sleeping with her boss, who was married, was more information than anyone needed. Even the girls. If worst came to worst, she still had her gun. She rubbed her bare arms with her hands, suddenly chilled.

"No. I have no intention of going back down that road again," she finally said. "Once was one time too many."

"That's good to know. Look, I'm really sorry about putting him on you like that. I had no idea."

Stephanie waved off her apology. "You had no way of knowing. It's not your fault."

"I'll keep my eye out for him should he ever come back."

Stephanie nodded absently then turned to Elizabeth, worry etched on her face. "What if he does come back? What if he starts trouble? What if any of the clients start trouble? We never even thought about security for the place."

"You're absolutely right. We didn't even discuss it."

Stephanie sighed. "Now more than ever we should. I'll look into some security firms first thing in the morning."

"I can take care of that. I'll ask Ron. I'm sure he can recommend someone."

"Good. And the sooner the better."

"I'm sure Ann Marie and Barbara will agree."

"We'll discuss it all at closing. I have some potential job candidates that I want to run past everyone and hopefully we can get the interview process started immediately."

"Can we hire on the spot?" Elizabeth moaned. She craned her neck and rotated her shoulders.

Stephanie laughed. "If only it were that easy. We definitely want to check and double check references. Can't have just anyone working here."

Elizabeth groaned. "Yeah, I guess you're right. Anyway, let me get back up front." She went for the door. Stephanie was right behind her.

"Can't say this place doesn't keep you on your toes," she said.

Elizabeth chuckled. "So true."

When they came back to the front of the spa, two new clients were waiting at the check-in desk. Dawne was working on getting them set up and Ann Marie had taken over in the exercise room.

"I'll go down and check the sauna room," Stephanie said.

"I'll go up to the lounge."

The two separated and went about the business of keeping their newly formed empire running.

Stephanie ran smack into Barbara as she was

exiting the massage room. They both grabbed each other to keep from tumbling backward.

"Wow."

"Ouch."

"Sorry," they said in unison.

"Where are you off to in such a blind hurry?" Barbara asked, tugging on her white smock.

"Huh?"

Barbara peered at Stephanie a little closer. "Are you all right?"

Stephanie finally focused on Barbara. "Yeah, uh, I'm fine." She shook her head and forced herself to smile. "Just a bunch of stuff on my mind."

"Anything I can help with?"

Stephanie drew in a breath and let it out slowly. "I wish. I got myself into this mess; I'll get out of it."

The two inches between Barbara's brows drew together in a tight line. "Got yourself into what?"

"I guess you'll find out soon enough." She pursed her lips. "Conrad was just here."

"Say what!"

Stephanie nodded.

"What did he want? I know he ain't thinking about joining," she said with a snap of her neck.

"I don't know what he was thinking about but he was here."

"Well what did he say? Did he bother you,

threaten you?" She reached out and put a hand on Stephanie's shoulder.

"No, nothing like that."

"You're shaking." She took Stephanie by the arm and steered her into the empty massage room. She shut the door. "What's going on girl? You know you can tell me."

Stephanie lowered herself into the chair, clasped and unclasped her hands until they started to sweat. In a series of fits and starts she told Barbara what happened to her that night in her apartment.

Barbara took it all in without saying a word, hiding her fury beneath a calm mask. How dare that bastard violate her that way and then have the nerve to show his face! Poor Stephanie. No wonder she is always two seconds from exploding.

Stephanie wiped tears away with the back of her hand and sniffed hard. She looked across at Barbara through bleary eyes. "Please don't say anything."

"Of course not. But Steph, you can't let him get away with that. He raped you."

Stephanie visibly shuddered. She wrapped her arms around her body and slowly rocked back and forth in the chair. "I could have stopped him," she murmured like someone coming out of a deep sleep.

"How? He's a grown man who apparently had one thing on his mind. How were you going to stop him?"

"I have a gun."

Barbara's hand flew to her mouth to stifle the gasp. "What?" she hissed, her eyes wide in shock. "Are you crazy?"

"I think I could have done it," she said so softly Barbara wasn't sure she'd heard her.

"You think you could have done it," she repeated. She craned her neck forward. "You would have actually shot the man, maybe killed him. That's what you're saying?"

Stephanie looked away, tugged on her bottom lip with her teeth.

"Steph." Barbara came from behind the desk and bent down in front of her. "Look at me."

Stephanie glanced up.

"This is serious hon. A helluva lot more serious than some fling with your boss. And now he's showing up here." She shook her head. "He has to be stopped." She jumped up.

Stephanie grabbed her by the wrist. "Barbara, please, leave it alone. I can handle Conrad."

"With a gun!" Her expression was a roadmap of worry and concern, veering off in several directions at once.

"We're going to get security for the spa. I've had my locks on my apartment changed and I'm going to change my number."

Barbara paced. She wondered if Stephanie had enough skill to put a positive spin on the police carting her away after shooting her ex-lover. Lawd. She pushed out a heavy breath.

"Look, I want you to promise me that if he even thinks about coming near you, making threats or making you feel uncomfortable in any way you go straight to the police. 'Cause, Steph, I swear to you, if you don't I will. And you know I'll do it. I love you girl, and I'm not going to sit back and let something happen to you."

That declaration set off a new bout of tears. Finally Stephanie pulled herself together. "I'll be all right." She sniffed and snatched a tissue from the box on the desk and wiped her eyes and nose. "And I'll follow your advice. I promise."

Barbara gave a short snap of her head. "And get rid of that gun."

Chapter 11

Ann Marie stepped outside of Pause and began walking down the street to where she'd parked her car. The meeting she'd just left with the girls still had her head spinning. The very idea that Stephanie was perhaps being stalked by her ex-lover was unnerving to say the least. Although she didn't go into details, Ann Marie was sure that there was more to the story than Stephanie was telling and it was pretty clear Barbara knew more than she let on.

She took a quick glance over her shoulder—just in case—and tucked her purse more securely beneath her arm. You just never knew when a lover was going to flip, she thought as she disengaged the alarm on her car. One minute they could be the most sweet, loving person you'd ever met, the next a stalker or worse—a long lost husband who wasn't lost at all.

She got in the car and pulled off several moments later. When she came to a stoplight, her cell phone rang. Without looking at the number she reflexively pressed the telephone icon.

"Hello?"

"So you weren't going to return my call?"

The center of her chest knitted into a tight knot. "Terrance." She blew out a breath. "What is it?"

"Why did Raquel move out and into an apartment?"

"What does that have to do with you?" Her temples began to pound.

"She's my daughter, Mari."

"It hasn't mattered to you all these years. No sense in claiming to care now."

"You took that option out of my hands a long time ago when you stole my daughter and disappeared."

Her heart raced at an unnatural clip. "Stole your daughter!" She laughed to keep from screaming. The light turned green. She stepped on the accelerator with such force she shot through the intersection, her tires screaming.

"It was wrong Mari. You know it was wrong. No one has the right to steal a child from its parent. All those years I can never get back—we can never get back."

"Don't try to make me feel guilty, Terrance. Don't you dare." She turned the corner on two wheels, screeching to a halt at the next light.

"It broke my heart."

Her throat clenched.

"You never knew that did you?" The lilt of his voice caressed her in hidden places.

She swallowed. Her eyes stung. "It was a long time ago, Terrance."

"But I haven't forgotten. You were the only woman I ever loved, Mari. No matter what you may think."

"I don't want to hear this, Terrance. Not now. It's too late."

"It's never too late to make amends."

Her hands were shaking. She put the car in Park, squeezed her eyes shut. "It is too late," she murmured. "I'm not the same girl."

"Yes, I know. And I can't wait to see the woman you've become. You remember how it was between us, Mari?"

Her nipples hardened as she stifled a moan.

"Do you?" he whispered in her ear.

"I…I have to go."

"I'll see you soon."

The call disconnected.

Her body trembled with a need she'd kept in abeyance. Just his voice, just the mere mention of what they once had turned her into a cat in heat.

Focus girl, focus. Put Terrance out of your mind. You have a date with a great man. Terrance Bishop is the past. Sterling Chambers is the present and maybe the future. Focus. She repeated the mantra all the way to her apartment.

Ann Marle made quick work of taking a shower and changing into a pair of jeans and a freshly starched white blouse. She freshened her makeup and fluffed her shoulder-length hair. She'd just purchased a pair of three-inch heels made of denim that she'd been dying to wear. This was the perfect outfit. She checked her appearance in the mirror. Satisfied she hurried out. Baring any late evening traffic, she should arrive at Sterling's place right on time.

Sterling opened the door and a slow smile of appreciation spread across his mouth. His dark eyes rolled down her body then up to her eyes. He leaned forward and put a light kiss on her lips.

"Hey." He took her hand and ushered her inside. "Welcome."

"...to my lair said the spider to the fly," she joked.

Sterling chuckled. "Naw, nothing like that. Come on in and make yourself comfortable. Dinner is almost ready."

"Can I help with something?"

"This is your night. Maybe you can do the honors next time."

"Love to."

"Want a drink?"

"Sounds good. What are you having?"

"Brandy."

"I'll take a short one with ice."

"Coming right up." He walked toward the bar on the far side of the simple but totally contemporary living room.

Ann Marie followed him into the room and looked around. He definitely had good taste, she observed. Understated and classy.

The butterscotch colored leather sectional looked soft enough to melt in your mouth. A low, smoked-glass table and two smaller matching ones were the focal points of the room, that is until she noticed the entertainment unit. It rose almost to the cathedral ceiling and was at least six feet in width. A state-of-the-art stereo system sat on the top of the multilevel unit. Set directly in the center was a plasma-screen television, the size of which she'd never seen before. One vertical cabinet held an innumerable amount of CDs and actual albums. The other cabinet held DVDs and VHS tapes. He certainly must like music and movies, she thought.

She walked around and took in the two art pieces that hung on the wall. Both were abstracts in brilliant colors with a focus on the butterscotch color of the sectional.

"Here you go," he said, coming up behind her with her drink.

She turned and took the drink. "You have a great looking place." She sipped her drink.

"Thanks." He glanced around absently. "It's comfortable." He walked over to the stereo, lifted a remote control and turned on the music. Kem drifted sensuously into the room. "So, how did everything go today after I left? You all looked pretty busy." He walked toward the couch and sat down.

Ann Marie took a seat. She smiled. "We stayed busy right up to closing." She shook her head slowly. "It's really quite incredible how well things have taken off." She leaned back against the plush leather. "Terrance called," she said softly and glanced at him above the rim of her glass.

"Oh." His eyes jerked in her direction then away. "What did he say, if you don't mind my asking?"

"He wanted to know why our daughter Raquel moved out."

His brows rose. "Why did she move out?"

Ann Marie looked away. "It's a long story."

"We have the whole night."

She sighed then leaned back in her seat. "She moved in a few months ago. Left her husband. Or should I say her husband left her—for another man."

"Whoa. One of *those* brothers."

"Seems so. When she left she came to me. It was hard at first. Raquel and I have…never been very close. But then we seemed to be making some headway. She helped out a great deal with the opening of the spa. I found out things about my daughter that I'd never known." She smiled sadly. "Then this thing with her pops…"

He sipped his drink thoughtfully. "But that doesn't explain why she moved out."

Ann Marie stood and walked toward the bar, thought about refreshing her drink but changed her mind. She kept her back to Sterling. "We had a falling out about her father." She turned to him. "I'd rather not talk about it if you don't mind."

Sterling blew out a breath. "Done. If you want to…I'm always willing to listen."

She nodded. "Thanks."

Sterling got up. "Dinner should be just about ready." He walked to the kitchen. He turned off the oven and opened the door, pulling out the pan with the steaks and baked potatoes. What had happened? he wondered as he put the tray on the counter. He wanted to get to know Ann Marie. But the more he found out, the less he actually knew. Maybe getting involved with her and all her issues was more than he bargained for.

He took two plates out of the over-the-sink cabinets and placed them on the counter. But there was something about Ann Marie that moved him. For all of her tough exterior there was a softness underneath that longed to come out. He wanted to be the one to open that door. Terrance Bishop, he thought, spooning the food onto the plates. What kind of man was he that could leave such an impact years after he'd been long gone? It was clear that he still shook Ann Marie. Was her reaction to him simply one of old memories and bad vibes or did she still care about the man she remained married to?

He walked into the living room with the plates. When he saw her standing in front of the windows she looked so tiny and vulnerable. He was going to make it his business to wipe Terrance Bishop out of her mind and, if need be, out of her heart.

"Dinner is served, Madame," he said in a very bad British accent.

Ann Marie turned, a gentle smile on her face. Sterling's insides shook just a little. Yes, he was going to make her forget.

"We can eat in here." He placed the dishes on the table. "I'll get the salad."

"I'm impressed," she said crossing the room and sitting on the couch.

Sterling winked. "I have all kinds of skills and talents."

"I'm sure." She spread the napkin on her lap. "Is this something you do for all your lady friends?" She cut into her tender steak.

He shrugged slightly. "I don't make it a habit if that's what you're asking."

She put a piece of steak in her mouth and chewed thoughtfully. "It seems that you know all about my dirty laundry and other than where you work and live I know nothing about you."

He grinned. "I'm used to being the one who asks the questions." He wagged a finger playfully at her and did a pretty good imitation of Al Pacino as Michael Corleone in *The Godfather*. "This one time I'm going to let you ask me about my business."

Ann Marie cracked up laughing. "If you ever quit your day job you could do some stand-up."

She put down her fork and wiped her mouth. "Well have you ever been married, have any kids?"

"No to both questions. I'm an old-school brother. I have no intention of putting the cart before the horse. I want the wife first then the kids." He paused a moment. "To be truthful I'm not really interested in a wife either."

His answer was surprising to Ann Marie. She wasn't certain if she was disappointed or not. "That's honest," she said.

"I guess it's because I didn't have the best of role models. My mom and dad had what you would call a dysfunctional marriage. It ended ugly and the ugly ending was the best part. The years getting there..." He shook his head slowly, frowning as the past entered his present. "I grew up thinking that *bitch* and *no-good bastard* were terms of endearment, that the Saturday-night boxing matches weren't only reserved for television. I got the live broadcast right in my house." He sighed heavily. "We were poor. I mean really poor. The kind of poor that sits by the window and waits for the welfare check. The kind of poor when your vocabulary only consists of four-letter words and your only form of entertainment is to sit on a bench and watch the world go by while you cuss it out for not including you on the trip.

The kind of poor when you believe that the only way out is down, and drugs and violence are the quickest way to get there." He looked into her eyes. "I saw and heard things growing up that left a stain on my soul that I don't think I'll ever be able to remove."

"I'm sorry. I shouldn't have asked."

He held up his hand. "No. It's okay, really." His features went through a series of movements. "After dealing with that for years, it hardened me in a way. I never attached myself to anyone. Whatever I did was for the moment—immediate gratification. I guess it came from being deprived of so much for so long. I just want to gobble everything up as quickly as I can and move on." He reached for his drink on the table and took a long swallow. "Pretty shallow, huh?"

"Not at all. We all have pasts that color our present. What and who we are today is made up from all the little pieces we picked up along the way."

"Sounds very wise," he said with a sad smile.

"Don't know about wise, but I do know that it's true. The trick is to be able to see all that and learn from it. Some folks are luckier than others in that regard."

"What have you learned from your past?"

Ann Marie lowered her head then looked directly

into his eyes. "That no matter how far and how fast you run, your past will always catch up with you."

They were both silent as they listened to their pasts tapping gently on the door, begging to be let in.

Chapter 12

"You have to let me help clean up," Ann Marie said, picking up the dishes to take them into the kitchen. "It's the least I can do after such a nice meal."

"On one condition."

She looked at him askance. "What condition?"

"That you let me take you out again."

Ann Marie drew in a slow breath. Sterling's words were so simple but the sincerity in his eyes and timbre of his voice elevated the simplicity to much higher implications.

"I'd like that very much."

He pressed his lips together and nodded then started toward the kitchen. "I was thinking that you might want to take the next thing smoking after hearing my confession." He glanced at her over his shoulder as he bent to open the dishwasher.

"Me don't scare easy," she said, slipping her accent back in place. "Got to come betta den 'dat. Besides what woman don't really want a bad boy wrapped up in a good suit?" With her hand on her hip she looked him up and down.

Sterling laughed long and hard. "Woman, you are something else."

"So I 'ere." She winked.

Sterling walked up close to her. "That's what I like about you," he said in a rough whisper.

"What's that?"

He grinned. "That…something else." His gaze held hers for an instant before he lowered his head to touch his lips gently to hers.

Ann Marie drew in a short, startled breath, the contact sending a shock through her body.

Sterling pressed closer, his arms snaked around her small waist. He let his tongue drift across her mouth until it opened ever so slightly and welcomed him inside.

Her tongue did a slow, tentative dance with his,

feeling her way, matching her step to his. She moved closer while his fingers played along the curve of her spine.

This was by no means her first kiss, Ann Marie thought as the warmth flowed through her veins. But everything about it was new, exciting and full of possibilities.

By degrees Sterling eased back. He brushed his thumb across her mouth. "That was nice."

"Yeah, it was." She lowered her gaze then looked up at him. "So…now what?"

"It can be whatever you want it to be." He moved further away and leaned against the counter, looking at her. "I have to be honest with you."

Her heart knocked against her chest. She didn't know what to expect.

"I haven't been in a serious relationship in a very long time, for a number of reasons." He cleared his throat. "This isn't going to be easy for me."

"What isn't going to be easy?" she asked, hesitation drawing out each word.

"Getting into a serious relationship."

"Are you thinking about getting into a serious relationship with me?"

His mouth quirked into a semi-smile. "I think so."

"Funny, I'd been thinking the same thing about you."

He smiled full out. "Is that right?"

"Yes." She suddenly felt like a young thing. "That's right."

Sterling reached out and stroked her cheek with the tip of his finger.

"Even with all you know about Terrance?" She held her breath.

"We'll deal with it when the time comes. My gut feeling is that he wants to finally break ties— once and for all."

Ann Marie looked up into his eyes, wishing that she could believe in what she saw there. She still held onto some secrets; the delivery of flowers, Terrance's declaration of love and the heat she still felt deep in her belly for him.

She rose up on tiptoe and tenderly pressed her lips to Sterling's. If she let him, if she let herself, she could push Terrance and all that he represented behind her.

Sterling held her close. There was less than a breath separating them. He lifted her ever so slightly off her feet so that each dip and every curve of their bodies melted into each other like pieces from a puzzle.

This was so unlike him, he thought as his arousal grew and pulsed, seeking release. He tread the relationship road with caution. Women came in and out of his life as often as the mood hit him. There'd been no one to captivate his full attention. They were all either looking for a quick diamond ring or a sugar daddy with no strings. He wasn't into playing either role. He was in love with the law and his music.

Slowly he put Ann Marie on her feet.

"Woman…" He smiled down at her. "You could make a man change his mind."

Ann Marie cocked a brow. "Really? About what?"

"About slowing down and taking in the view."

"What's stopped you from slowing down before?"

He turned away, suddenly subdued. "Let's go inside."

Ann Marie wasn't sure what had happened as she followed him into the living room. That's when she noticed a saxophone resting in a stand against the wall.

"You play?" she asked pointing to the sax.

The smile returned to his face. "As often as I can."

"You keep surprising me. First you cook and now you play." Her eyes ran over him. She drew in a breath and let out her question. "What just happened back there? Just like that," she snapped her fingers, "you…changed."

Sterling strolled over to the floor to ceiling windows and stared out onto Central Park. "I guess you could say I have a tug of war going on."

Ann Marie lowered herself onto the loveseat, preparing for anything. She folded her hands in her lap and waited.

He turned to face her, slid his hands into the pockets of his slacks. "When we met," he shrugged, "I figured it would be something casual. You know." He tugged on his full bottom lip with his teeth for a moment. "Getting all serious was not on the docket. But then spending time with you, getting to know you, all the rules are starting to change. And then there's the issue about your husband."

Her mouth pinched. She lowered her head then looked directly at him. "I can't give you any guarantees. I have a lot of baggage. Some I can leave at the door, then some I have to drag in the house with me."

He flashed a crooked grin. "All I'm saying is that as much as I want to jump feet first into this thing with us I know that if I do I'm going to be all tied up in you woman."

She rose slowly from her seat and crossed the room to stand in front of him. "When we met, you know the thing that struck me about you? You said you liked a challenge."

"I did, didn't I?" He brushed his thumb across her lips and she captured it in her mouth. "You are definitely that and more." He lowered his head and kissed her, tenderly at first and then with more urgency.

Ann Marie rose up on tiptoe and wrapped her arms around his neck, sinking into the warmth and security of him.

"Are you sure?" he whispered against her mouth.

"Can one ever be fully sure about anything," she whispered back.

He took her by the hand and led her to his bedroom.

Once inside Sterling dimmed the lights then took her in his arms once again. He knew making love with Ann Marie could only lead to trouble but he didn't care. All he cared about at the moment was possessing her, feeling her wrapped around him, succumbing to her island fire.

He unbuttoned her blouse and pushed it down over her arms then tossed it on a chair by the window. Then he unfastened her jeans.

Ann Marie stepped out of her shoes and took off her jeans. Her lime green ensemble was near iridescent against her rich brown skin.

She was a perfect little package, Sterling thought taking in her delicate curves. And her skin felt like silk as he ran his hands along her exposed flesh. He slipped his hands behind her knees and around her waist and picked her up then carried her to the king-sized bed. He gently put her down and lay beside her taking in every inch of her with his eyes.

Ann Marie felt suddenly shy, as if this was her first time, hoping and praying that he liked what he saw. She'd never before second-guessed her effect on a man. This time she did. This time it mattered.

He pushed one strap down off her shoulder then the other. His fingers caressed the crest of her breasts. She shuddered beneath his touch. He stroked her cheek. "You're beautiful you know."

"Am I?"

"Yes…you are."

His hands trailed across her stomach and he felt the muscle quiver. He let his fingers run beneath the band of her panties…teasing.

She worked to unfasten the buttons of his shirt then played with the hard muscles of his chest. But what she wanted to touch was below, pulsing against her thigh. She reached down and massaged the bulge in his slacks. He drew in a sharp breath.

"Look at me," she whispered as she stroked him.

Sterling looked into her eyes, his own hot and needy.

Ann Marie unzipped his pants and released him into her hand. Sterling groaned with pleasure as her warm palm wrapped around him. She stroked him, up and down, slow and deliberate. Sterling's eyes squeezed shut as the rippling sensation rushed through him.

He pushed her bra aside and captured a rising nipple in his mouth. Ann Marie gasped with pleasure, cupping his head to draw him even closer. She stroked him harder and felt the beginnings of his eruption dribble across her hand. He grew even harder and longer if that were possible.

She had to have him. Damn the consequences. Damn tomorrow and damn Terrance. She pushed his hand deeper into her panties and he fingered her until her body was a mass of shudders.

Sterling flipped her fully onto her back. He looked down into her wide eyes as he pulled her panties down. She wiggled out of them and spread her legs bending them at the knees. He settled himself between her tight thighs, bracing his weight on his forearms. His tongue licked across her mouth, nibbled her bottom lips. She arched her hips. He pushed against her feeling her wet heat but didn't move inside her, just teased her with the tip of his penis. She whimpered with need.

He reached across to his nightstand and took out a condom then reared back on his knees and slowly put it on. As Ann Marie watched, that moment was suddenly the most erotic thing she'd witnessed.

Sterling tossed the empty packet to the floor. He reached forward and cupped her breasts in each hand and gently squeezed. She shut her eyes but they flew open when she felt the pressure of him opening her up as he pressed inside her—slow, determined, harder than steel.

Ann Marie drew in a breath that she couldn't release when she felt him fully inside her. My God it felt so good, so right, so complete.

He grabbed her apple bottom and pulled her upward, impaling himself so deeply inside her not even air separated them.

And then they found that beat, that perfect rhythm that was like no other dance. It was purely theirs, something that could not be imitated or duplicated. They refined their step, created new ones without losing a beat.

Sterling didn't just do the sex thing, he made love to her entire body with his hands, his mouth, with whispers of endearment, words of encouragement, telling her what he wanted, asking what he could give her until it was more than either of them could stand.

They moved faster, rotating hips and locking lips, picking up the beat until they both erupted to an explosion of tribal drums that pounded and vibrated through every muscle of their bodies.

Ann Marie trembled as Sterling held her tight, burying his face in her neck. He placed tender kisses there even as her insides still quivered, released and contracted around the fullness of him.

Sterling was stunned. He'd lost count of the number of women he'd bedded over the years. For the most part one blended into the other until they all seemed the same. Ann Marie didn't fit into that category. He'd expected their lovemaking to be a great experience, but this…this was something else. It was exactly what he'd been afraid of all these years. What was he going to do now?

Ann Marie sighed softly. She could still feel him inside her and not only in the physical sense but that place deep inside her soul. The only other person who'd touched her there had been Terrance. Since the day she walked out on him, she only dreamed that some other man would be able to make her feel the way that Terrance had. She'd come close on occasion and thought for sure that she would finally be able to exorcise Terrance from her mind and body. It had never happened—until tonight. But she dare not cling to this feeling or else fall victim once again to that kind of power.

Slowly she released her legs from around his waist and wiggled from beneath him.

"Are you okay?"

"Mmm, hmm," she murmured.

Sterling reached over and pushed the damp hair away from her face. Briefly she turned to look at him then glanced away.

Sterling rose up on his elbow and stared down at her profile. "What is it Ann Marie?"

She pushed up from the bed, grabbed the sheet and wrapped it around her diminutive body. "Nothing. Really."

She walked toward the bathroom and shut the door behind her.

Sterling flipped onto his back and stared up at the ceiling. What had just happened? Where had the woman gone that was so hot for him? He almost felt as if she was going to toss some money on the dresser and wish him goodnight. He clenched his jaw.

Maybe it was all for the best, he reasoned. It was never his intention to get involved in the first place. It was just one of those things. Nothing more. But if that's all it was why did he feel like he wanted so much more?

His gaze shifted in the direction of the bathroom when he heard the shower come on. He sat up in bed, wrapped his arms around his drawn up knees. She was washing him off her body, but something deep in his gut let him know she would not be able to wash him out of her soul, at least not without a fight.

When Ann Marie emerged from the bathroom she had a towel wrapped around her. She looked everywhere in the room except at Sterling, but that didn't keep him from watching her. She silently gathered up her clothes and took them to the far side of the spacious bedroom. She kept her back to him as she got dressed.

Sterling watched the scene unfold with disbelief clouding his vision. Was she actually going to walk out—just like that? That was his routine.

Ann Marie stepped into her shoes, still without a word.

"Is this your usual M.O.?" Sterling finally asked.

Her head snapped up. "What do you mean?"

He got up from the bed, naked as the day he was born and strode across the room to stand in front of her. He lifted her chin with the tip of his index finger, forcing her to look him in the eye.

"I mean do you generally go to bed with men and then get up and walk out without a word? Is that how you operate?" His dark eyes raced over her face.

She snatched her chin away. "I don't know what you mean. I'm going home—where I live. I didn't know there was a law against that."

"You know perfectly well that's not what I'm saying, Ann Marie."

"What ya won me say? It was good for me, too?" she snapped.

"Yeah, maybe I do," he said softly, his voice filled with such blatant sincerity, it stopped Ann Marie short. She dared to look at him.

She swallowed. His eyes welcomed her.

"It was," she whispered.

"Is that a bad thing?" he asked, his tone soft and cajoling.

She nodded her head. "It can be. For me it can be." She folded her arms as if to protect herself from him.

Sterling reached out to her. His strong fingers wrapped around her arm. "It can be for me, too, Ann," he confessed. "I'm just as afraid as you are."

She slowly gazed up at him, her wide eyes luminous and uncertain. "Don't play me the fool."

"I'm not." He unwound her arms and pulled them down to her sides. "I want to give us a try, Ann Marie. A real try. And trust me, I don't say that easily." He ran his tongue across his lips. "I know we have a bunch of stuff to get through before we can really see the future clearly. But I think we can do it. If you want to."

"Do you really mean that—or is it just good sex talking?" She offered up a wicked smile.

Sterling grinned. "Hmm, good sex does have a way of clouding one's judgment." He rubbed his chin in thought and Ann Marie poked him in the ribs. "Seriously, though." He chuckled and threaded his fingers through her hair. "Let's give it our best shot. At least we'll know that we tried."

She thought about how she felt when she looked at him, when he smiled, when he held her, when they made love. She knew that Sterling had cracked open the door that had remained sealed for a long time. Even Phil had not been able to get through the barricades that she'd set up around her emotions.

The safest thing to do would be to leave now, cut this thing off before she got so entangled she couldn't break free. That way they could both walk away with their feelings and their dignity intact. It wasn't fair to Sterling to get involved with him while her situation and feelings for Terrance remained unresolved.

She pressed her palms against his chest. "I've got to go. I have a long day tomorrow."

The stunned expression on Sterling's face froze his features. Before he could recover, she reached for her purse on the chair next to her and walked toward the door.

"At least leave my money on the table on your way out," he shouted to her retreating back.

Her step faltered for an instant but she kept going, knowing that if she stopped, if she turned and looked into his eyes, she would be lost.

She opened the front door and walked out, closing it softly behind her.

Sterling picked up a glass from the nightstand and hurled it across the room.

Chapter 13

Sterling couldn't remember the last time he'd been so pissed off at a woman. For the most part he'd never cared enough to give a good damn about what they thought, felt or wanted.

He pulled his Navigator into the parking garage next to the building that housed his law office. He barely spoke to the attendant as he usually did each morning, sharing a few barbs about whatever sporting event happened to be on the air the night before. He may have grumbled something as he tossed his keys and slammed the door shut to the oversized vehicle. He couldn't be sure. He'd been unable to focus in on a clear thought since Ann Marie walked out on him two nights earlier.

Walked out on *him!* The whole concept was so foreign to him he'd actually scratched his head in disbelief.

He stepped out of the garage and right into a slushy puddle of icy, dirty water. A violent string of expletives shot from his mouth causing a female passerby to jump away in alarm and hold her purse close to her chest.

"Dammit!" he spat one last time, looking down at the mess that was now his shoes and the hem of his Hugo Boss pants. He turned right and pushed through the revolving doors of the building.

A blast of heat hit him in the face in sharp contrast to the biting chill of outside. A thin coating of snow had fallen over night but of course the streets of Manhattan, hot from the massive flow of human traffic and the underground subway system, were no more than a slush fest.

Sterling pressed the button to the elevator and hoped that he had an extra pair of shoes in his office. The elevator door opened and his buddy Nick stepped off.

"Hey man. How's it going?" Nick asked, tucking his black cashmere scarf into his coat.

"Awright."

Nick frowned. "Don't sound awright," he tossed back in Sterling's same monotone. "Tough case?"

"Something like that."

The elevator dinged.

"There's a gig on Friday night at Innervision. You in?"

Sterling nodded. "Yeah, sounds good. What time?"

"First set is eight."

Sterling nodded. "I gotta run. Have a case I need to go over."

The elevator doors slid shut.

"Shit," Sterling spat. He kicked the elevator door.

Nick grabbed Sterling's shoulder and peered into his face. "What's with you? I know it's not some case," he said keeping his voice low.

Sterling blew out an exasperated breath, rocking his jaw back and forth. "Nothing. Nothing."

"Bull. I know you better than that." Nick glanced around. "Come on, you run your own show. You can get in when you damn well please. Let's throw back some java and chill for a minute."

Sterling's face was a mass of ticks and frowns. His shoulders slumped. "Yeah, awright."

The two men headed out, dodged traffic and darted across the street to Starbucks.

"Want something exotic or straight up no chaser?" Nick asked as they stood in line.

"Straight for me," Sterling muttered.

Nick stole a glance at him over his shoulder but Sterling's gaze was off in the distance.

Nick ordered two black coffees and walked with Sterling to a table in the back. He put the cups in the center of the table.

Sterling went for his without a word and tilted the steaming brew up to his lips.

Nick winced, knowing how hot it was, and Sterling didn't flinch. He waited a few beats before attacking the matter at hand. "So you want to tell me what bug you have up your ass this morning? And don't tell me its work."

Sterling pursed his lips in thought. He put the cup down, glanced out the window at the pedestrians hurrying by. He and Nick had been friends since law school. But what brought them together was their love of music. Sterling had spotted Nick one night in one of the local Georgetown jazz clubs in D.C. while they were both attending George Washington University. Nick was playing with a small band and Sterling was truly impressed with the brother's skills. After the last set he went up to him and introduced himself, told him he played sax. The rest, as they say, is history. Nick hooked him up with the band he played with and they'd been buddies ever since.

But they were more than legal colleagues, with Nick practicing corporate law, and they were more than music lovers. Nick was the one true friend Sterling had. He was the only person that he ever shared anything personal with and the same was true of Nick. However, it was Nick who was the most settled of the two. Nick was a solid, married man with two kids and a wonderful wife who was forever trying to hook Sterling up with any one of her eligible girlfriends, much to Sterling's amusement.

"You can't keep running the streets forever," Nick would regularly remind Sterling. "One of these days the right one is going to come along and blow your natural mind."

Seems like "the day" had arrived.

Sterling sighed, turned away from the window and reached for his coffee cup. "It's this woman," he finally said.

Nick's brows flicked upward but he remained mum.

"Met her a few weeks back. Beautiful, sexy, intelligent, fiercely independent." He paused and looked at Nick. "And dynamite in bed."

"Sounds like the whole package. So what's the issue?"

"She's not feeling me."

"Really? And you know this how?"

"She walked out on me." He snapped his fingers. "Just like that. And right after the most mind-blowing sex." He shook his head. "I still can't believe it."

"Sounds like you got a dose of your own medicine my man. Or maybe your game is falling off."

Sterling shot him a look of venom. "That ain't it. Trust me."

"So then what is it?"

"She's married."

"Whoa!" Nick jerked back in his seat. "You're tapping a married woman?" He leaned forward. "Are you crazy?"

"It's not like that."

"Oh yeah. So what's it like then, Sterling?"

"They haven't been together in over twenty years. He lives in Jamaica."

The skin between Nick's brows bunched together. "Twenty years. Hmm. So what is she doing about it?"

"That's the thing. After all this time, her husband locates her and wants to see her...and their daughter."

Nick blew out a breath from between puckered lips. "This is definitely a two-cup conversation…"

Over the next hour Sterling spilled out the story of his meeting Ann Marie, his initial intention of hitting and running, getting caught up in her sensual web and how his mind and heart were now twisted out of shape.

"Wow," Nick said when Sterling finished. "Sounds to me that you may have met your match my brotha. Have you called her since the other night?"

Sterling shook his head no. "Lost count of how many times I picked up the phone and put it back down. I don't want her to think for a moment that I'm sweating her, you know."

Nick chuckled. "But you are."

Sterling grimaced. "Very funny."

"Hey, my advice, give the woman a call. Maybe she got scared. All sorts of things could be going through her head. She may be thinking that you may not want to speak to her now. But you'll never know if you don't call her. The worst thing that could happen is that she tells you it's not going to work. And if she does, at least you will know how to move on. But rolling like this will make you crazy."

"Yeah…maybe." He finished off the last of his

second cup of coffee. He nodded his head. "But what if she says get lost?"

Nick tipped his cup in Sterling's direction and raised a brow. "Then beat it." He chuckled lightly and Sterling smiled for the first time in days.

Ann Marie had taken the day off from the real estate office to work at the spa. She was tired of Carol asking her what was wrong. Since she'd left Sterling's apartment she'd been a mental mess. Every inch of her wanted to stay, to cuddle, to enjoy the pleasure of being with a man that she truly cared about. But she was so torn. How could she get involved with Sterling, risk her heart and her emotions, when things were still so unsettled with Terrance? It wasn't fair to Sterling to drag him into the quagmire of her life, especially when she couldn't be certain why her heart was skipping a beat when she heard Terrance's voice or thought about the time they once shared. But she couldn't stop thinking about Sterling and how free she felt when she was with him.

She was staring at the blank computer screen when Stephanie walked up to the front desk.

"Hey Ann, what has your lip hanging?"

Ann Marie's eyes rose slightly. She shrugged. "One of dem days."

Stephanie leaned with her elbows on the counter. "Which one is it?"

"Huh?"

"Terrance or Sterling?"

Ann Marie pouted. "Both. Well sort of." She sighed heavily. She turned to Stephanie and looked her in the eye, kept her voice low. "I slept with him the other night."

"Oh," Stephanie said, wide-eyed. "Well…"

"Well what?"

"How was it girl?"

Ann Marie giggled. "Loss for words."

"You? I don't believe it. That good huh?"

"Better."

"Dayum." She thought for a moment. "So what's the problem?"

"Don't think I should get involved with Sterling until I clear up this mess with Terrance."

"Never stopped you before."

"This is different."

"How?"

Ann Marie struggled to put her emotions into words that made sense. Every scenario she came up with sounded juvenile and naïve. "I care about him."

Stephanie's expression twisted. "Color me slow, but is that really such a bad thing, Ann?"

"For me it is." She shook her head. "I can't go

down that trail again. Falling in love, being committed, really caring about another person."

"But Ann, that's what being in love is all about."

"Not for me. I lose myself. I lost myself with Terrance and it damn near ruined me for good. Maybe it did." She raised imploring eyes to Stephanie. "And I know if I give in, the same thing will happen with Sterling."

Stephanie steepled her fingers in thought trying to make sense of Ann Marie's logic. Here she was with two men who obviously cared about her and apparently gave it to her so good she turned into putty. Most women would give their two front teeth to be in Ann Marie's shoes. But if anyone knew the devastation brought on by becoming sexually addiction to someone it was Stephanie. Especially when it was the wrong someone.

"Sis, listen to me. Sterling is not Terrance. What Terrance did or didn't do, you have to let it go. You'll never know what the future will hold if you won't kick the past to the curb. Take it from someone who knows. Conrad had me hooked, not only sexually but financially, as well, and it took him raping me to make me finally open my eyes to what I was doing to myself." She took a breath. "But then I found Tony." A slow smile bloomed across her polished mouth. "And it's all good. But you have to be willing to take that chance." She covered Ann Marie's hand with her own. "Call him," she said softly.

Ann Marie pushed her lips together.

"You know you want to talk to that man."

Ann Marie smiled. "Yeah." She dragged out the word like the last note of a song. "I do."

"Then call the brother."

The front door opened and Tony peeked his head in and waved.

"Duty calls," Ann Marie teased.

"We're going to see *The Color Purple*." She put on her coat and tucked her purse under her arm.

"Have a good time."

"I will."

Tony walked up to the desk. "Hey Ann, how are you?"

"Not bad. Busy, but that's a good thing."

"I see some new faces."

"Yes we hired four people in the last week. Two massage therapists, a front desk hostess and a trainer for the exercise rooms. Tomorrow I'm scheduled to see three people for the café." She turned to Ann. "Oh, and a guy may come in tomorrow, a Drew Hawkins. He was the one referred by Ron to do security."

"Security?" Tony quizzed.

Stephanie heaved a breath, thought about dancing around the truth and decided for the time being that was the best option. "Yes, we decided that we needed it. We can't be too careful."

"That's true. Hey, we better get going or we'll be late."

"See you tomorrow, Ann." She lowered her voice. "And don't forget what I said." She mouthed, "call him."

"Have a great time you two." Ann Marie chuckled as she watched them leave. It was still hard to believe that with all the bad vibes that had existed between her and Stephanie for years, they were ultimately the ones each other turned to. Funny.

She turned the computer screen toward her and pulled up Sterling's profile. For several moments she simply enjoyed looking at his picture. He did say he loved a challenge, she thought. She was happier with him than she had been for a long time. He knew about Terrance and was still willing to try to work things out. He was good to look at and great in bed and, as usual, when she was backed into a corner by emotion, she turned into a bitch.

Sterling didn't deserve that. She reached for the

phone and dialed his number. Hopefully, if and when he answered, she would have figured out something to say.

* * *

"Oh my goodness," Stephanie gushed as they exited the theater. "It was absolutely incredible." The light of her smile was like a beacon as they walked arm and arm down the street. "The singing…" she pressed her hand to her chest. "Makes you want to run out and go to church or something."

Tony chuckled. "It was good. I'm glad you enjoyed it."

"I can't thank you enough. I had an unforgettable time. Wait till I tell the girls. They are going to be soooo jealous." She giggled.

"You're going to rub it in their faces?" he asked pretending to be appalled.

Stephanie jerked her head to the side. "I sure am. They all have a man. Let their man take them like mine did." She hugged his arm tighter.

He looked down at her. "I'm your man." His tone wavered between a statement and a question.

Stephanie stopped walking and looked directly into his eyes. "Yes. You're my man." She reached up and kissed him on the lips. "Don't forget it," she said against his mouth before stepping back.

"That would be pretty hard to do with you being my woman and all." He grinned.

"Let's go home," she said, the three simple words full of invitation.

"You won't get an argument from me."

"Make yourself comfortable," Stephanie said. She took his coat and hung it up in the hall closet. "Thirsty?"

"No, I'm good." He walked into the living room and sat down.

"I'm going to change I'll be…" The ringing doorbell cut her off in mid-sentence.

Tony glanced over his shoulder toward the door as Stephanie went to answer it. She pulled it open a bit and drew in a sharp breath.

"What are you doing here?"

"Aren't you going to invite me in?"

"No. Leave. Now."

"Steph, what's wrong?"

She turned halfway. Tony got up from his seat and came toward her.

"It's okay, Tony."

"Tony! Who the hell is Tony?"

Chapter 14

Conrad looked Tony over, sizing him up. He spoke through clenched teeth. "This is none of your business."

"If it has to do with Stephanie it *is* my business. I'm pretty sure she asked you to leave. I won't be so nice."

"Are you threatening me?"

"Take it anyway you want." Tony took a step forward. Stephanie pressed her palm to his chest.

"Did she tell you about us?" Conrad taunted.

Tony's eyes widened for a split second. "No need. There's nothing to tell. Now leave."

"I want you out of here Conrad," Stephanie shouted. "Do you understand? Now!"

Conrad's face went crimson. The veins in his neck pulsed. "This isn't over until I say so," he spat, wagging a finger at Stephanie.

Tony lunged for him. Stephanie stepped up and shut the door seconds before Tony grabbed Conrad. She quickly locked the door.

Tony's chest heaved in and out. His nostrils flared. "Who the hell was that?" he shouted pointing to the door.

Stephanie paced in a small circle, biting down on her thumbnail. "My old boss," she mumbled.

"What?" He craned his neck forward in disbelief.

She swallowed. "Come inside. There are some things I need to tell you."

Tony sat down with his arms draped across his knees, his head lowered as he listened to Stephanie's sordid tale of her affair with her boss.

"I know it was stupid to get involved with him…he's married."

Tony's head jerked up but he remained quiet, knowing that if he said something he would lose it.

"At first it was just about the sex," she admitted and flinched when she noticed the tight expression on Tony's face. "But as time went on and I got promotions and higher commissions, it all helped to take care of my sister Samantha. I felt trapped. I knew if I broke it off he would blacklist me in the industry. Then what would I do?" Her eyes begged him to understand. "Then when my friends decided to open the spa I saw it as my way out. I broke off the relationship and quit my job." She blew out a breath. "But he refuses to accept that it's over. He came to the spa the other day. That's why we got the security," she admitted.

Tony ran his tongue across his lips and slowly shook his head. "Why didn't you tell me all of this before?"

"I...I knew...I thought you would think the worst of me."

He was silent for a long time. Stephanie's heart raced. She twisted her hands in her lap.

"We all make mistakes. Most times we think that they're for the right reasons." He looked at her. "Come here," he said softly.

Timidly Stephanie came to stand in front of him. He took her hand and pulled her down to sit beside him.

"Is that everything, all of it?"

She nodded. It was everything. Everything except the rape. She wasn't ready to tell him that, not yet, maybe never.

He gathered her close. She rested her head on

his strong shoulder. "You're going to get a restraining order against him. I'm going with you. And you're going to stay with me for a while especially after he gets served. I'm not taking no for answer. I don't want you to think about it. Just get your things together."

Stephanie was so stunned she couldn't react. This was a brand new Tony. Not the easygoing, fun-loving guy she'd met in a diner to discuss brochures.

"I don't know what to say."

"There's nothing for you to say unless you disagree." His gaze didn't falter.

"Tonight?"

"We can stay here tonight. It's late. Tomorrow we go down to the court and file the order and tomorrow night you stay with me."

Slowly she nodded in agreement. "Okay."

He stroked her hair. "It's going to be all right. I'm not going to let anything happen to you."

She'd never had a man stand up for her, want to protect her. The men in her life had all wanted something. If it wasn't sex it was what she could do for their careers. This was all so new and scary.

"Why are you crying?" He tilted her chin upward and wiped a tear from her cheek.

"I don't know. Overwhelmed I guess." She sniffed and laughed nervously.

He kissed her forehead. "You don't have anything to worry about. I'm here."

That only made her cry harder.

"Steph," he held her closer. "What is it? Tell me."

"I…it's been so long…" she sniffed and wiped at her eyes. "That I've had someone…" her voice broke into little pieces of pain, "take care of me." Her body shuddered as she tried to hold in her sobs and failed.

Tony held her tighter. "Sssh, it's okay babe. You have me now. And I'm not going to let anyone hurt you ever again," he breathed into her hair. "Never. Understand?"

She bobbed her head up and down against his chest. Tony caressed her back soothing her like you would a wounded child.

Stephanie always came across to him as totally together, tough and resilient. This was a side of her he'd never seen or imagined: soft, dependent and vulnerable. Right at that moment he wanted to be able to shut out the world, stomp out all those who'd caused her a moment of anguish and make everything right in her world. He was falling for Stephanie. The truth was he'd already fallen. Hard. When that guy showed up at her door something inside of him snapped. He wasn't naïve enough to believe that Stephanie didn't have a life before they'd met. But he didn't want her past in his face. And from tonight on, he'd make sure it wasn't in hers either. If she let him, he knew that he could make her happy, make her forget all about the past and heal all of her wounds. Tonight was a new beginning for them both.

"Tony..."

"Hmmm."

"Make love to me."

He pulled back and looked down at her. "Are you sure?"

She nodded. "Very."

His eyes slowly rolled over her face, looking for any signs of doubt or hesitation.

She leaned upward and kissed him. He ran his fingers through her hair and pulled her closer. She parted her lips and let him in. Their tongues danced slowly together, in and out, exploring.

Stephanie moaned softly when his hands trailed down her back, playing along her spine. She arched forward, needing to be closer. She fumbled with the buttons of his shirt, finally opening it. Her fingertips grazed his chest down to his belly. She felt the muscles there shudder beneath her fingers.

"Not here," she whispered against his mouth. She eased away and stood in front of him. She pulled her T-shirt over her head, unzipped her jeans and stepped out of them.

"You're beautiful," he murmured. His eyes ran a hot path along the length of her curves.

She stretched her hand out to him. He took it and followed her into her bedroom.

For Stephanie everything moved in slow motion, like a movie, frame by frame. She captured it all. Each kiss, each touch. Tony was gentle, patient, willing to take eternity if it would make her happy.

They tumbled onto the bed, legs, arms and mouths entwined, unwilling to let even a breath of air separate them.

Tony unfastened her bra and freed the heaviness of her breasts. A sharp intake of breath filled the air when his tongue laved over one taut nipple then the other. His fingers strolled along her waist until they reached the band of her thongs and pushed them down. Somehow she managed to wiggle out of them and kicked them to the side of the queen-size bed.

He tore off his shirt and tossed it to the floor then quickly returned his mouth to hers. She sucked on his bottom lip while she worked to unfasten his pants. The kiss grew more frenzied as he pumped against her. He got out of his pants and boxers and they both gasped in stunned surprised when their bare flesh came fully in contact with each other.

He pushed her legs apart with a sweep of his leg and rested between her thighs. She bent her knees and Tony cupped them above his arms, raising her legs until they braced his shoulders.

Her heart raced furiously with anticipation. The pulsing head of his penis beat against her wet opening, longing to be filled.

Tony snatched a pillow and shoved it under her hips, raising her even higher. He looked down into her eyes. Her lips parted. The air caught in her throat. The sensation of him entering her stilled her heart. Her stomach quivered. He pushed a little more. More. He groaned. Stephanie's head rocked back and forth. His hands held her hips, immobilizing her as he pushed in and out, slow and steady.

Stephanie's mind spun. Her body desperately needed to surge against Tony's. But he wouldn't let her. It was deliriously maddening. He raised her legs higher; draping them around his neck then spread them high and wide. Tony rotated his hips.

"Tony!" Her neck arched.

He got on his knees still holding Stephanie's legs wide open. He jammed into her until they both shuddered. He did it again and again.

"Ooooh…" Stephanie moaned.

"Give yourself to me," he urged.

Stephanie's gaze met his demanding one. She pushed hips upward. Tony sucked in air from between his teeth. Stephanie smiled. She squeezed her inner muscles. Rocked her hips. She cupped her breasts in the palm of each hand offering up the fruit to Tony. She clenched her muscles again. Tony shivered, lowered his head and took one nipple into his mouth and feasted.

Stephanie moved in slow circles beneath him. Then faster, faster. Their breathing escalated in syncopated rhythms until it became one unified high note that shattered into millions of bright lights and bursts of electricity that shot through their veins.

"Agh," Tony growled as he surged into her, his spine freezing as life shot out of him.

"Ooohmygod," Stephanie wailed. Her insides clenched in a wild frenzy. Her body shook uncontrollably.

Tony squeezed her to him, burying his face in her neck. Stephanie wrapped her limbs tightly around his body, binding him to her until the last of their vibrations were spent.

Stephanie slowly lowered her legs, the muscles screamed. She snuggled against Tony. He brushed her damp hair away from her face and kissed her tenderly on her cheek.

"In the morning," he said his voice raw and gravelly, "pack a bag. We can come back for anything else that you need." He kissed her lips.

Stephanie locked her fingers behind his head and nodded. "Are you sure?"

"Never more sure about anything." He eased off her and lay on his side facing her. Stephanie draped her arm across his waist. "I want you to be just as sure."

Stephanie swallowed. If she did this, took this leap, she would once again be putting her well-being in the hands of a man. She looked into his searching eyes. Is that what she really wanted?

"I'm sure," she said, the words, soft but strong.

"Steph…"

"Hmm?"

"We didn't use protection."

She drew in a slow breath and looked into his eyes. "I know."

Chapter 15

"It's been a rough week," Ellie said. She lifted a cup of coffee to her lips. "Thank goodness we finally got the extra help."

"I know. We couldn't have held up much longer." Barbara chuckled and took two English muffins out of the toaster then put them on a plate on the island counter. Sunday morning gospel from WBLS FM played softly in the background.

"Butter or jelly?"

"Cream cheese."

Barbara shook her head and grinned. Elizabeth

loved cream cheese and would look for any opportunity to lather it on something.

Barbara got the butter, jelly and cream cheese from the fridge and put them on the table. She took a seat opposite Elizabeth, wrapped her hands around her mug of coffee and looked across at her friend.

"I never told you about Wil Hutchinson," she began before spreading grape jelly on her muffin.

Elizabeth frowned for an instant and shook her head. "No, I don't think so. But…" she pointed a finger toward Barbara. "Isn't that the guy who came to the spa?"

Barbara nodded.

"I thought there was something going on there, but…" She shrugged. "So what's going on?"

"Wil and I met in high school. Then we both attended Howard University together."

Elizabeth relaxed in her seat.

"When I saw him again, everything came rushing back like it was yesterday."

Elizabeth smiled. "So you two must have been pretty hot."

"More than that. We were in love. Really in love. We had plans." She gazed off into the distance.

"So…what happened?"

"I got pregnant."

Elizabeth's eyes widened. "Pregnant?"

Barbara nodded. She pressed her lips together. "He left you because you got pregnant?"

"No. I left him."

"Barb, I'm not understanding. Start from the beginning."

She drew in a long breath and slowly exhaled. "Wil and I originally met through a friend in high school. He was the captain of the football team. The minute I saw Wil, you know that funny feeling you get in the pit of your stomach?"

Elizabeth bobbed her head up and down.

"Well I got it…bad." She laughed lightly.

"Gurl." Elizabeth rocked back in her chair and slapped the table with her palm. "I sho' nuff know that feeling," she said, thinking of when she saw Ron for the first time.

Barbara laughed as the joy of those days washed over her. "Anyway, we really hit it off from the beginning. Every girl in school wished she was me."

"I hear ya."

"Wil was a year ahead of me. He went onto Howard and I swore that I was going to follow him there as soon as I graduated."

"Which you did."

Barbara sighed. "My parents were so strict. I was an only child and a girl. My father was a Pentecostal minister."

"I never knew that."

"Religion was his world, almost to the exclusion of everything else. I didn't have a social life unless it had something to do with church. No boyfriends, no dating."

"So how did you manage to get involved with Wil?"

"Sneaking around. My friend Margaret, the one who introduced us, would cover for me. She was the only person that my parents trusted me to be with." She chuckled. "I'd tell my parents that we were doing work in the church or at the library. Once I was able to get away, I'd meet up with Wil." She closed her eyes for a moment. "I was so in love. When he left to go away to school I truly thought I was dying inside. It was the longest year of my life. My folks were dead set against me going away to school. Told me no good would come to me in some big city like Washington or New York. They wouldn't hear of it."

"So how did you manage to get into Howard?"

"I worked after school and every single day during the summer. Saved every dime. I bought a train ticket from Walterboro South Carolina to Washington, D.C. for the next to the last week in August. I never told my parents." She swallowed. "I just got on that train and went to see Wil."

"Barbara, you didn't tell your parents? They must have been frantic."

"I wrote them and told them I was safe. Didn't give them a return address or anything."

"But...where did you live?"

"Wil had a small studio apartment off campus. That's where we lived. I worked during the day while Wil went to school. I saved my money to pay for two classes the next semester. That's when I found out I was pregnant."

Elizabeth reached across the table and covered Barbara's hand.

"I was terrified. I didn't know what to do. I was too afraid to tell Wil. I couldn't go home. I knew having a baby would ruin everything for Wil. His plans and dreams of going into the NFL would have come to a halt." She clenched her hand. "So I ran. Wil went to school one morning and I left. I came to New York."

"But what happened with the baby?"

Barbara bit down on her bottom lip. "I got a room at the local YWCA and started hunting down clinics that would...help me."

"Barb, you don't have to tell me anymore."

Barbara held up her hand. "No. I want to. I need to. I've held this in for so many years." Her eyes cinched at the corners. She stared into Elizabeth's eyes. "You're the first person I've ever said anything to about this." She was quiet for a moment, feeling for the words, hoping they didn't still hurt as deeply when she said them aloud. "I went to the clinic. The women there were so helpful and sympathetic to me. They gave me several options. They would help me find housing and a part-time job and I could raise the baby myself as a single mother or I could put the baby up for adoption." She shook her head slowly.

"When I walked in there all I wanted was for it to be over. I didn't want to have to think about it for a minute longer than I had to. But the thought of going through with it…or giving my baby up to strangers, never knowing it or it knowing me…or raising it alone at nineteen…" Her voice cracked with pain. She wiped her eyes. "I felt so trapped." She looked into Elizabeth's eyes, the haunting agony still evident. "I took the information with me back to the Y, to think about it, you know." Elizabeth held Barbara's hand as if to give her strength. "Life is funny. When you can't make a choice it just steps right in and makes it for you. I went to bed that night and when I woke up I was in the hospital."

"What? What happened?"

"Sometime during the night I started bleeding.

The pain was excruciating. I was able to make it to the bathroom in the hallway that was shared on my floor. That's the last thing I remember."

"Oh, Barbara, I…I'm so sorry."

"When I woke up my mother was sitting in the chair by my bed."

Elizabeth gasped.

"She said I could have come to her even though my father never wanted to see me again." Her short laugh was an empty sound. "She stayed until I was released from the hospital then she went back home. The doctors told me I'd had an entopic pregnancy and probably wouldn't be able to have children."

Elizabeth lowered her head, not able to imagine how devastating that news was to someone so young.

Barbara drew herself up. "Anyway, a few years later I met Marvin." She shrugged. "And the rest you know."

"Did Marvin know?"

Barbara shook her head. "We simply resigned ourselves to not having children. What has haunted me all these years was that after I left the clinic, I'd made up my mind to go through with having the baby and taking care of it myself. A part of me always felt that I was being punished for even thinking about taking a life."

"You don't really believe that do you?"

"Years of being browbeaten by religion does things to you. I would say a million prayers for forgiveness anytime Wil and I would make love. I just knew I was going straight to hell. I guess my penance was never being able to have children of my own."

"Barbara, we all make mistakes. Especially when we're young. If there is one thing that I believe it's that God is a merciful God. Bad things happen to good people all the time."

"I suppose." She looked at Elizabeth. "So there you have it, my sordid, dark past." She brought the mug to her lips and took a sip. "And now my past is right here in front of me once again."

"How do you feel about Wil?"

She tugged on her bottom lip with her teeth for a moment. "Honestly?"

"Yes, honestly."

"I never stopped loving him. Never."

"Then you have a decision to make my friend."

Barbara looked off into the distance then down at the diamond sparkling on the third finger of her left hand. "I know."

Wil finished his mail route and returned to the main post office to check out. He couldn't remember what he did for the entire day. All he could think about was Barbara. He still could not believe that after all these years he'd run into her again.

He returned his mail cart and punched out. Stepping out into the chilling November air he took a look around as if seeing the city he'd lived in for years for the first time. He zipped up his wool jacket and hunched his shoulders against the stiff wind and started home. Since his wife died, he'd resigned himself to being alone, at least with regard to a relationship. His focus had been on raising Chauncey to the exclusion of everything else. Now, with his son on the threshold of stepping out into the world on his own, he would really be alone.

Was Barbara seeing anyone? Had she ever married? Did she have children? She was still just as sweet and as beautiful as he remembered. But with that memory came a pain he'd never quite gotten over—the day she disappeared.

She was simply gone as if she'd never been there. He'd come home from class, excited about having an NFL scout check him out at practice. They wanted to talk, but he wanted to talk to Barbara first. If he did get drafted to the NFL he wanted them to be married first. He'd come home ready to pop the big question…

His throat tightened as the images of an empty

apartment suddenly loomed before him. All that was left of their relationship was a cursory note. "It's best this way. Please don't look for me. Barbara."

To this day he couldn't understand why she'd done it. How could she have hurt him that way? For months he'd walked around in a trance, barely getting through his days. It effected his playing and ultimately cost him everything.

The team had been in the middle of a scrimmage. He couldn't concentrate. He went out to receive a pass and the next thing he knew he was crumpled in a heap, his right leg twisted at an odd angle. Any thoughts of going to the NFL were shattered just like his leg.

The bus pulled up to the stop and Wil got on board. Stepping on, he found a seat in the back. He stared out the window as the bus rumbled down Amsterdam Avenue and images of those painful days rolled by and how his love for Barbara turned into something ugly.

While he lay in the hospital with a series of pins and braces on his leg he hated her. Hated her for leaving him, hated her for loving him, hated her for taking away his dream.

It was Kimberly who'd nursed him back to health, stuck with him through rehab and helped to mend his broken heart. So he married her. In a way it was to thank her for being there for him. He couldn't say he truly loved Kim because in his heart, as much as his anger tarnished the image of Barbara, he knew he'd never love anyone other than her.

It wasn't fair to Kim. He knew it but he couldn't help it.

"She's gone, Wil. Gone," she'd said time and again. "When are you going to let it go? I'm you're wife, the mother of your child, but all you care about is Barbara!"

He had no answer for her. It was true. And then one day Kim couldn't take it anymore and she walked out.

The bus came to his stop and he pulled himself up from his seat and got off.

As the years passed and as Chauncey grew, Barbara got pushed to the back of his mind. His anger and disappointment had waned over the years. And then there she was.

He turned the key in his door. He had to find out what happened back then. She owed him an explanation.

Chapter 16

Sterling had been thinking about his conversation with Nick. He was no punk and he certainly wasn't afraid of some woman's scorn. He pushed papers around on his desk.

Why had Ann Marie gotten under his skin the way she had? What was it about her that was so different from any other woman he'd tapped?

Everything.

He blew out a breath of exasperation.

It wasn't supposed to go down the way it had. His feelings weren't supposed to get all twisted out of shape. But they had.

He hadn't slept a wink since she'd left and concentrating on the case file in front of him was out of the question. He flipped the folder closed and pushed back from his desk.

He stood, grabbed his coat from rack by the door and headed out. He was going to treat Ann Marie like one of his cases. He intended to win.

This time when he arrived at Pause he was surprised to see some new faces, the most prominent being a very buff man who was seated near the door.

"Good afternoon, welcome to Pause. Do you have your membership card, sir?" the man asked.

Sterling wrinkled his face for a moment and glanced at the name tag on the muscular chest. Drew Hawkins. Sterling dug inside his suit jacket and extracted his wallet. He flipped through his array of credit cards until he found his spa membership. He showed it to him.

Drew looked at the card then at Sterling. He nodded and handed it back. "Enjoy your stay. Be sure to check in at the front desk."

Sterling mumbled under his breath while shoving the wallet back in his pocket. He crossed the entry foyer to the reception desk. Again he was met with a new face. This name tag read Tina.

She beamed at him. "Good afternoon. Are you a member?"

"Yes."

"Great!" she chirped. "May I have your card to sign you into the system?"

He went through the process again. Tina put his information into the computer. She stared at the screen a few moments then handed back his card.

"I see you don't have an appointment for any of our special services. Would you like to schedule a massage?"

"No. Thanks. Actually, I'm looking for Ann Marie."

"Oh. Let me page her." She picked up the phone and called for Ann Marie to come to the front desk. "She should be here shortly."

"Thank you." Sterling leaned against the counter while he waited for Ann Marie to appear. Then he turned to Tina. "Who's Mr. Universe at the door?"

Tina grinned. "That's Drew Hawkins, security."

"I didn't realize the spa needed security."

Tina shrugged. "I just started three days ago. He was here when I got here."

"Hmm."

He glanced toward the café and saw Ann Marie coming in his direction. When she saw him, her steady gait faltered for a moment. He saw her lift her chin then continue toward him.

"Sterling," she said by way of a greeting.

"Can we go somewhere and talk?"

Ann Marie snatched a glance at Tina who was pretending not to be eavesdropping. "We can talk in the office," she said barely above a whisper, then turned and headed for the stairs.

The office door was open. Ann Marie walked in, stood to the side to let Sterling pass then closed the door behind him. She crossed the room.

"I wasn't expecting you," she said, keeping her back to him.

"I'm going to get right to the point."

She turned slowly toward him, keeping her eyes level with his.

"I will admit that when we first met, it was all about just checking you out and moving on. Finding out about Terrance should have sealed the deal for me. With any other woman it would have." He slid his hands into his pockets, his expression stoic. "But something happened Ann Marie." He looked directly at her. "The game I'd been playing with relationships wasn't all that it was cracked up to be. I want more. I want you."

Ann Marie didn't know where to look. She wanted to believe him. She wanted to give in and simply let the relationship go wherever it was meant to go. But if it did, she was certain she would fall victim to the weakness of her heart.

She dared look at him and in that instant she was lost.

"I'm afraid," she whispered.

Sterling took a step toward her then another, until he was right up on her. He lifted her chin with the tip of his finger. "Look at me." She did. "So am I," he confessed.

A shaky smile formed at the corners of her mouth. "How are we going to do this?"

"Slow and easy." His gaze darkened with mischief.

Ann Marie ran a finger down the center of his chest. "I like the sound of that."

Sterling lowered his head until his lips were inches away from hers. He hesitated a moment, cupped the back of her head in his palm and pulled her forward.

The kiss set her on fire. She felt her entire being engulfed in heat. Her heart pounded in her chest. She rose up on her toes and instinctively her arms wrapped around his waist sealing his body to hers.

Her mind warred with her heart. Instinct told her to run, leave this man and all the complications that came with him alone. But her heart, her spirit, needed what Sterling offered her—a chance—a chance at real happiness.

With much reluctance Sterling eased back. He

stroked her cheek. Damn he had it bad for this woman. She'd worked some kind of magic on him. He knew what he was letting himself in for, but he didn't care. All he knew was that for as long as time allowed he wanted her in his life. Somehow they'd work out all the rest. They had to.

"I'd better go."

All she could do was nod her head.

"I'm playing tonight at the Lennox Lounge. I'd love it if you came."

Her eyes brightened. "Really? What time?"

"First set is at eight."

"I'll be there."

He grinned like a kid. "Great." He leaned down and pecked her lightly on the lips. "Maybe I'll even play something for you."

"I'd like that."

He took a step back. "I'll see you later."

"I'll be there."

He turned to leave then stopped at the door. He glanced at her over his shoulder. "No more running." He opened the door and walked out.

Ann Marie slumped down in the chair and nibbled on her recently manicured nail. He'd come for her, she thought. It didn't matter to him about Terrance. He wanted to be with her, work things out. This was her second chance and she was going to take it.

"Oh there you are."

Ann Marie glanced up to the open door. "Hey Barbara."

Barbara stepped in, a stack of towels in her hand. "Everything okay? You look a little dazed."

Ann Marie smiled. "I think I am, chile." She leaned back in the chair and told Barbara about what had transpired from the night she walked out on Sterling to his declaration a few moments ago.

Barbara slowly shook her head. "Sounds like you have a good man there, Ann. We're not young chicks anymore. Our chances at happiness and finding *the one* gets slimmer and slimmer." She thought about Michael and Wil. "Sometimes we have to step out on faith, you know."

"That's what I'm going to do. Step out and take my chances."

"That'a girl. Well, I better get to my clients. Talk to you later. Have a ball tonight."

Ann Marie smiled. "I intend to."

Finding parking in the heart of Harlem on a Friday night was always a task. But with the resurgence of the famed area of Manhattan, complete with restaurants and clubs, it was more difficult than usual. Ann Marie circled around for a good twenty minutes before she finally found a space. She walked back the block and a half to reach the Lenox Lounge.

She stood in line behind at least a dozen others waiting to get in. She could hear music coming from inside each time the door opened and wondered if Sterling was playing already. The line inched along. She pulled up the collar of her mink coat against the biting wind that had suddenly kicked up and looked skyward. The forecast predicted a possibility of snow and she only hoped it would hold off long enough for her to at least get inside. She shivered a bit and pulled her coat tighter around her body.

Finally she reached the front door and stepped inside to be greeted by a warm blast of air and a thin layer of cigarette smoke. The Lenox Lounge had always been one of Harlem's hot spots. At one point or another all the greats had played there. Over the years as Harlem declined, the influx of musicians dwindled. But with Harlem now being the place to be once again the nightlife was back in full force, which was obvious from the crush of people trying to squeeze their way in.

Ann Marie wound her way around the dressed to impress bodies in the dimly lit interior and was able to find a table in the back of the club.

Before she got herself good and settled, a

waitress stepped up to her table to take her drink order. Ann Marie asked for an apple martini then took in her surroundings.

The band that was playing finished up their set and the MC for the evening took the mic to announce that there would be a twenty-minute intermission and the marquee band for the evening, After Hours, would take the stage.

A tune by Miles Davis played in the background underscoring the bubble of laughter and conversation that floated around her. It was extremely rare that Ann Marie went out alone. She was accustomed to being accompanied by a man. Looking around her she felt out of place and hoped that the single men who hung together in groups of twos and threes, and periodically looked her way, wouldn't get it in their heads that she was out scouting.

The waitress returned with her drink and asked if she'd like to order an appetizer. She presented a short menu. Ann Marie looked it over in the dim lighting and selected buffalo wings and a small side salad. She flashed a tight smile as she handed back the menu.

There was a sudden flurry of activity on the stage and she looked up and caught a glimpse of Sterling as he took up his position. She watched him through the crowd. Finally his eyes landed on her and a full-blown smile illuminated the darkness. He put his sax down on the stand and hopped off the stage, bounding over to her table. He slid into the seat next to her and planted a sweet juicy one on her lips.

"Hey," he said against her mouth.

"Hey yourself." She brushed her lipstick from his lips with the pad of her thumb.

"Glad you could make it."

"I told you I would."

"Yo, Sterling!"

Sterling glanced toward the stage. He was being waved over. "Gotta run. The show must go on." He pecked her on the lips and hopped up.

Ann Marie watched him set up and suddenly felt a wave of pride. That was her man up there. *Her man.*

The M.C. stepped up on stage and gave a glowing introduction, highlighting After Hours as a favorite of The Lounge and announcing their recently released CD, which would be available after the show.

"Sit back relax and enjoy the musical stylings of After Hours."

The six piece band: drummer, bass, piano, guitar, trumpet and sax players moved into an easy Ellington favorite *Take the A Train,* which got the crowd immediately into the music.

Ann Marie's food arrived but she was so taken in watching Sterling do his thing, she forgot all about it. The first hour set flew by and during the brief intermission, Sterling came and sat with her for a few minutes.

"During my solo," he said before running off for the last set, "I'm going to play something just for you." He squeezed her hand and returned to the stage.

And he did. It was the sweetest most soul-stirring version of *A House is Not a Home,* that she'd ever heard. Every wailing note cried out to her, embraced her. The music poured out of his instrument as clearly as it poured out of his eyes that stayed trained on her as he played. Sterling's alto sax was so crisp, the notes so clear you could actually hear the words as if they were being sung.

Her heart swelled with joy. She felt like crying from happiness.

When he finished his solo, the tight room was wrapped in awed silence. And then as if on cue, applause rose like thunder until every inch of space was filled with adulation.

Sterling took a bow in Ann Marie's direction and tipped his sax at her. More than a few heads turned in her direction. She felt her face flush with warmth. She returned his salute with a coy smile.

The band stepped off the stage and mingled

with the crowd. Sterling came over to her table and sat down.

"So what did you think?"

"You can give up your day job anytime." She laughed lightly.

"I'll take that as a compliment." He reached across the table and covered her hand with his. "I'm really glad you came."

"So am I."

He stared into her eyes. A flurry of emotion ran through him. He wanted her—in every way—not just sexually. The realization settled inside him, finding a place in his spirit.

"I was thinking that maybe we could go to my place," his said, his statement laced with innuendo.

"Whenever you're ready."

"Let me go say goodnight to the fellas and then we can leave."

She nodded. The thought of having Sterling locked between her thighs had her pulse pumping double time. She knew it was risky, taking up with him. But what was life without a few risks? She was willing to take the chance.

Chapter 17

"Yes, this is Stephanie Moore," she said into the phone while discarding an application from a would-be employee. She'd just hired, with Barbara's approval, two new massage therapists. They still need at least two more people to cover the café.

"This is Terri Wells of Sterns & Blac."

"Hi Terri. What can I do for you?"

"I just wanted to bring you up to date on the Pause for Men campaign…"

Stephanie leaned back in her chair and listened. Several weeks earlier she'd been contacted by the PR firm to partner with them to create the Pause Man. It was a full-fledged campaign to promote the perfect man from the physical to the mental. Terri's plan included a workout regime, nutrition, finance management, grooming—everything to get a man into shape and ready for the perfect woman—all of which would be documented in a full spread in *GQ* magazine. The winner would go on the campaign trail, TV, radio spots and a major billboard in Times Square.

"Nike has come on board as one of the sponsors along with Delta Air Lines and Carol's Daughter with their bath and body line. We'll be using their product line throughout the campaign," Terri was saying.

"Carol's Daughter! That's great. I love their stuff. And whatever the men don't want the women will love!" she said, laughing.

"I know what you mean. I'm meeting with one of their reps today. What they plan to do is to create a Pause for Men package: soap, body wash, facial scrub, body oil and of course you will be able to sell it at the spa."

"Girl, you sure know how to work it."

"Gotta pay those bills."

They chuckled.

"How is the contest going?"

"Like wildfire. Everyone is signing up. Submissions end next week. I'll get them all together and send them over to you."

"Great. Well." She blew out a breath. "That's about it for now."

"We'll touch base next week."

"Sure. Hey, Stephanie…"

"Yes?"

"Um, have you ever thought of taking on a partner?"

"Partner?"

"Yes."

Stephanie frowned for a moment in thought. "Well…are you asking about yourself?"

"Yes."

"Has something happened?" She remembered her earlier conversation with Terri about her and her boss. She'd been down that slippery road before.

Terri hesitated. "It's something that I've been thinking about lately."

"We can certainly talk about it. Toss some ideas around."

"I think we would make a dynamic team."

Stephanie smiled. With someone as high octane as Terri Wells on her team they could easily compete with the big boys. "Let's make some time to discuss the possibilities after we get this contest out of the way."

"Fair enough."

"We'll talk soon. I—" A knock on her door interrupted her. She looked up, smiled and waved Ann Marie inside. "Sorry one of the co-owners just came in," she continued. "I'll get the entries over to you and we'll talk next week."

"Great. Have a good day."

"You too." She hung up. "Hey how are you?"

Ann Marie walked in and took a seat opposite the desk. "Pretty good." She grinned.

Stephanie monitored that smile. "Something's up," she hedged.

Ann Marie crossed her legs. "I took your advice."

"You took *my* advice." Stephanie tossed her head back and chuckled.

"Yeah, go figure." Playfully she rolled her eyes.

"So what great advice of mine did you take?"

"About me and Sterling."

Stephanie's brows rose. "Don't just sit there grinning. Tell me what the hell happened." She leaned forward eager for the blow by blow.

Ann Marie told her about Sterling's impromptu visit to her office and his invitation to the Lenox Lounge.

"Get out! He plays sax?"

Ann Marie nodded. "And damned good too, chile. He played a song just for me."

"There's something really sexy about musicians. And I love myself some sax players." She momentarily closed her eyes dreamily.

"Well this sax man is off limits. So don't be getting your panties in a bunch."

Stephanie chuckled. "Listen to you. Sounds like he did more than play the sax."

Ann Marie winked. "He did." She told Stephanie about going to his house afterwards, leaving out the very intimate details but giving enough information for Stephanie to get the lusty picture.

"I'm glad for you, Ann. Everyone deserves to be happy."

"I want this to work. I really do."

"But…"

Ann Marie looked away. "I don't want to screw up."

"Why do you think you would?"

Ann Marie didn't have a chance to answer. They both turned toward the door. Raquel and Terrance Bishop stood in the threshold.

Wil walked up to the reception desk. "Hi, I have an appointment for a massage," he said.

Tina looked up from the computer screen.

"Welcome to Pause. I'd be happy to help you. Your name please."

He gave her his name and she looked his appointment up on the computer. She printed out his card and handed it to him. "Let me tell Barbara that you're here." She called down to the massage room. "Your twelve o'clock is here, Ms. Allen."

Barbara squeezed the phone in her hand. She knew it was Wil. "Uh, Tina can you check with either Kayla or Sheryl and see if either of them can take him?" Kayla and Sheryl were the two new therapists that were just hired. Barbara crossed her fingers.

"Hmm, Kayla has a client now and one in an hour. Sheryl doesn't come in until three."

Barbara frowned. There was no way she could get out of it. "Okay. Give me a minute. I'll be right up."

Tina turned her smile on Wil. "She'll be right up. You can wait in the lounge or in the café."

"Thanks." He walked over to the seating area opposite the reception desk, sat down on one of the recliners and picked up a men's health magazine.

Barbara entered the reception area and spotted Wil right away. Her heart did that crazy dance thing in her chest. She drew in a breath and approached.

"Hi Wil. Sorry to keep you waiting."

Wil put down the magazine on the rack. "No

problem. I thought you were trying to pass me off to someone else." He grinned and she got hot all over.

"No, not at all. I didn't want you to wait." Her hands were shaking. She stuck them in the pockets of her smock. "If you're ready we can get started."

He stood and she was forced to look up at him. *God he still looked good.* Too good. How was she going to get through the next hour running her hands all over his body? Lawdhavemercy. "Follow me."

She led the way to the lower area and walked down the hallway to the massage room.

"There're towels and a robe in that closet," she said pointing. "I'll be back in a few minutes while you change. You can hang your things up in there as well. Take everything off," she added, the words almost sticking in her throat.

Their gazes caught and held for an instant too long. Barbara forced her feet to move toward the door.

Wil nodded as he watched her walk out. He unbuttoned his shirt and unfastened his pants. He'd spent a restless night thinking about today, what it would be like to have Barbara touch him again. There was a part of him that still ached for what she'd done to him—walking out of his life without a word of explanation—at least none that made sense to him. He should be angry, unforgiving. But instead, when he saw her again all he wanted was to turn back the hands of time, bringing back that time in their lives when the only thing that mattered to them was each other.

He hung his things up in the closet. Of course going back in time was impossible. They were different people now and the life they'd lived without each other had changed them both. He took off his T-shirt and shorts and put them with his clothes in the closet. He wrapped the towel around his waist and put on the terry robe just as Barbara knocked on the door.

"All clear," he shouted out. He tightened the belt on the robe.

Tentatively she walked in and shut the door behind her. She forced herself to look anyplace but in his eyes. "Come on. I'll take you to the shower first, then the steam room." She led him out.

While Wil was showering Barbara waited in the outside room, trying to compose herself. How was she going to manage this? How was she going to separate her warring emotions from her profession? She fingered her engagement ring that was tucked in her smock pocket. *You're engaged to be married to a wonderful man,* she reminded herself. *Michael loves you. You love*

Michael. You and Wil were a long time ago-ancient history. Don't forget that. She shut her eyes and repeated the mantra over and over. When she opened her eyes, Wil was standing in front of her.

Her gaze slowly trailed up from his bare legs to the towel tucked around his waist, to the glistening chest, up to his face and those eyes that she'd never forgotten. A soft smile touched his mouth. She drew in a breath.

"All done?"

He ran his tongue across his lips. "Yes."

She pushed herself up and found herself right up on him. He didn't move and she couldn't. He paused a beat then took one step back.

"After you," he said, his voice thick.

For a moment Barbara couldn't remember where the steam room was with him standing so close and looking at her as if she was the last supper. She blinked several times and got her bearings. She started off, stopped then turned in the opposite direction. "Sorry," she muttered feeling the heat of him right behind her.

She made it to the steam-room without any further flubs; got Wil settled, set the dials for twenty minutes and nearly ran out of the room to wait.

When he opened the steam room door twenty

minutes later, he emerged like a god from Greek mythology descending upon humankind from his throne above. To Barbara it was equivalent to watching a movie as he stepped through the steamy mists to stand before her. His body gleamed. Her heart thumped. She swallowed over the dry knot in her throat.

"Guess we should get you that massage," she said inanely. She stood on shaky legs and headed back to the massage room.

"Uh, just loosen the towel and lay on your stomach please."

She turned her back to him and prepared her massage oils and scrubs on a small rolling cart. "The spa has, uh, partnered with Carol's Daughter. We've been using their spa products. I'm sure you'll like them."

He rose up slightly and glanced at her. "You won't have me smelling like a girl will you?"

Barbara chuckled. "I'll try not to. Actually it's their men's line."

"Oh, good." He rested his chin on his crossed arms.

Barbara stepped up to the table and for a moment stared at the muscles in his back. Her gaze trailed down to the small chocolate birthmark on the left side of his spine. She smiled, remembering. She shook off the images and began opening bottles. She poured some oil on her palms and rubbed her hands together then added more.

She started at the base of his neck, massaging the muscles there. "Relax," she said softly, more for her benefit than his. She reached for his arms and guided them down to his sides. She worked his shoulders, his back, paying close attention to the knots of tension stored along either side of his spine.

Wil moaned both from the relief that ran through his body as from the heat of her touch. He closed his eyes while her fingers did their magic. He knew this was a professional experience. At least his mind understood that but his body said something completely different. Her fingers were sensual, waking him up, stirring him in ways that he'd held in check. As much as he wanted to think about cold showers and trucks, he couldn't. All he could imagine was Barbara touching him. It was Barbara, the woman he'd never stopped loving.

"You can turn over now," she said, sounding breathless.

He turned slowly. The towel caught around his hips as he did, revealing the soft hairs around his groin. Barbara's gaze, like a magnet zeroed in on his obvious erection.

"Barb," he whispered.

"Wil…I…"

He sat up and the towel fell away. He reached for her and she couldn't move. His hand clasped the back of her head and pulled her toward his waiting lips.

When his lips touched hers, fireworks went off in her head. Her heart thudded at a maddening pace. His left arm slid around her waist and she melted into his embrace.

Time spun backward. She was a young girl again and Wil was her first love. He kissed her with a passion and longing that she thought she'd found again in Michael. But she hadn't. This was it. This was it.

Wil held her tighter, afraid that if he loosened his hold on her this dream would slip away. Like a man half his age, he nimbly got up from the table, the towel now on the floor beneath his feet. He ran his hands along her back. He breathed her in, nuzzling her neck, the scent of her hair and skin like aphrodisiacs to his senses.

Barbara pressed against him, the feel of his arms around her, his strong naked body throbbing against hers, had her dizzy with desire. He groaned her name, turned her around until her back was now against the table. He bent her back until her body arched, her pelvis jutting out against his erection. His mouth slid down her neck. His fingers unbuttoned her smock and nearly tore it from her body.

All reason left her as she allowed him to undress her. The only coherent thought in her head was Wil, having him again, feeling him inside her again.

He lifted her onto the table and then climbed up, his heavy body hovering above her. He looked into her eyes. "I've never stopped loving you. Never," he groaned as he raised her knees up along his waist.

She couldn't breath, didn't want to. She felt the hardness of him press against her, demanding entry. God, she was so wet. Her body shook as he pushed inside her, just a little, teasing. She drew in a sharp breath as the length of him slowly filled her.

"Wil," she gasped.

His mouth covered hers, his kiss as deep as his entry into her body. They moved slowly, reacquainting themselves with each other, enjoying the reunion.

Barbara closed her eyes and held him, moving her hips against him, needing to feel every inch of him. They blended together so perfectly. If this is wrong, she thought in a haze, she didn't want to be right.

As their desire rose so did the tempo between them. Wil rocked in out of her, his mind totally scrambled. He was one giant raw nerve. He didn't ever want this to stop. But he knew that it would at any moment.

"Barb!" he ground out, surging against her.

She felt the muscles inside her suddenly contract and he cried out. Jolts of electricity shot through her. She buried her face in his neck as her body shook in uncontrolled release.

"Ohhh," she whimpered, shuddering as the last of her climax ebbed out of her.

They lay entangled with each other, their breaths coming hot and fast, slowly subsiding along with the beats of their hearts.

Wil stroked the sides of her face, brushing away the damp strands of hair from her cheeks. He tenderly kissed her lips.

"It wasn't what I thought it would be," he said.

Her breathing halted in her chest. She focused on his face.

"It was better." He grinned down at her and she giggled like a young girl.

She caressed his back and relaxed, letting her eyes drift closed. She should feel guilty, she realized. But she didn't. If anything, she felt gloriously alive, fulfilled and utterly satisfied.

Although so many years, so many experiences had passed between them since they last saw each other, they fit right back together like puzzle pieces. Perfect and complete. She held him tighter. But this couldn't happen again.

"I want to keep seeing you, Barb," he said against her neck. He rose up a bit and looked at her, waiting for a response.

"Wil…" She released her hold on him.

He eased up. She lowered her legs and sat up. Wil gave her some room. Suddenly she felt totally naked. Wil got off the table. She grabbed the sheet and pulled it up around her.

The intercom in the massage room blared.

"Ms. Allen, your next client is here."

Barbara's eyes flew to Wil's. He took the hint and went to retrieve his clothing.

"Are you going to talk to me?" he asked as he began getting dressed.

"Not now. I need to get ready." She quickly got dressed and wished she had time for a shower before her next client. She picked up her smock from the floor and her engagement ring fell out, rolled accusingly across the floor to stop at Wil's feet.

He stared at it a moment before bending down to pick it up. He examined it. His expression went from casual to concerned. He held it in his hands.

"Yours?" He held it out to her, watching her expression.

For a moment she couldn't move.

"Is it?"

The harsh bite of his question jarred her. She swallowed. "Yes." She took it from his hand and shoved it back in her pocket.

"You're married?" His voice held more pain than question.

"No." An eternity passed. "Engaged."

Chapter 18

Ann Marie was frozen in place. It had been more than twenty years since she'd set eyes on Terrance. Nothing about him had changed. If anything, his good looks had only ripened with age.

His presence sucked the air from the room and Ann Marie struggled to breathe.

Stephanie quickly took in the stark similarity between Raquel and the man standing next to her. There was no doubt in her mind that this was the one and only Terrance Bishop, the man Ann Marie had fled a country to get away from. Damn, damn, damn. "Do you want me to stay?" she whispered to Ann Marie.

Ann Marie slowly shook her head no.

Stephanie got up from her seat. "Good to see you again, Raquel."

"This is my father," she said, her voice laced with pride. She smiled up at her dad. "Dad, this is Stephanie Moore."

Terrance stuck out his hand and focused in on Stephanie. "My pleasure, Ms. Moore."

His accent was like music, a deep bass with wind instruments in the background.

Stephanie shook his hand, transfixed. "Nice to meet you." She turned to Ann Marie who had yet to budge. "I, uh, guess I'll go on upstairs." She turned back to Terrance and Raquel, started to walk out, when Terrance's voice stopped her.

"Sweetheart, why don't you go on upstairs and let your mother and I talk for a few minutes?"

Raquel tossed a sour glance in her mother's direction and reluctantly left with Stephanie.

Terrance turned all his charm on Ann Marie. "Still beautiful."

"Don't, Terrance."

He stepped closer. "Don't what—tell my wife that she's beautiful? What kind of husband would that make me?" He smiled down at her and she grew hot all over. "Mind if I sit down?"

"It wouldn't matter, I'm sure you'll do as you damn well please."

He chuckled. "Still fiery. I like that. I always liked that about you."

She turned away from him as he sat down. "What do you want Terrance?"

"To see you again. I told you that."

"Well, you've seen me. Now you can go."

"That's not all."

She flashed him a hard look. "What does that mean?"

"A reconciliation."

"You're crazy. It's done with us."

"Never."

The word vibrated inside her. He got up from his seat to stand directly over her. He took her hand and pulled her up from her seat. His arm snaked around her in a viselike grip. The room closed in around them. He lifted her off her feet to meet his lips. Her body shook.

"Terrance…" The word was a breath of air.

"Yes…" He lowered his head to capture her mouth.

She twisted her head away, but not before his hot mouth met hers for an instant too long.

"No," she said with little force.

He tried once more, clamping her head in his hand. His tongue darted in her mouth and her knees gave out. He held her tighter before slowly setting her back down on her feet. She pulled away, stumbling backward. Her eyes were wild, her breath escaping in uneven puffs. She looked up at him and a smile of achievement moved languidly across his mouth. He licked his lips. "Still sweet."

"Get out, Terrance." Her nostrils flared as she sucked in air.

Terrance made a move toward her, but stopped. "This isn't over between us, Mari. I'll be back." He turned and walked out.

Ann collapsed into the chair. She ran a trembling hand across her lips that still burned. She covered her face in her hands and wept.

"Engaged?"

The question hung in the air.

She nodded numbly.

"I see."

"Wil, I'm sorry, I should have told you."

"Yeah, maybe you should have." He brushed passed her and out the door without even a backward glance.

For several moments Barbara stood in the deafening silence. Then drawing in a breath she buttoned her smock and walked out and ran right into Stephanie.

"You'll never guess who was just here," Stephanie sputtered.

It took a moment for Barbara to register what was being said. "What?"

Stephanie repeated her statement then looked Barbara over. "Girl if I didn't know better I'd swear you just had a romp in the haystack."

Barbara inwardly flinched. "Who was just here?" she asked turning the inquiry away from her and her most current dilemma. She could still feel the beat of Wil inside her.

"Terrance."

Barbara frowned then her eyes widened. "Ann Marie's Terrance?"

"One and the same."

Barbara started off toward the office with Stephanie hot on her heels. Barbara knocked lightly on the door, her next client all but forgotten. When she didn't get an answer, she turned the knob and walked in.

Ann Marie was still at the desk. Her eyes were red and she was sniffling hard.

Barbara gingerly approached. "Ann," she said gently. "Are you all right?"

Stephanie looked around as if half expecting Terrance to jump out from behind a filing cabinet.

Ann Marie shook her head back and forth. Barbara eased over to her and pulled up a chair. "What happened?"

Ann Marie started blubbering and yammering in that accent that they couldn't understand, barely getting the gist of it out. In a nutshell, Terrance had reappeared and shook the foundation of her world with one unwanted but soul-shattering kiss.

"Damn him to hell," she finally spat.

Barbara and Stephanie looked at each other. With her sizzling tryst with Wil and now this thing with Terrance and Ann, she didn't want to imagine anything more.

Barbara took Ann Marie's hand and then Stephanie's just as Elizabeth walked in.

"Hey, what's going on? I swore I saw Raquel and a man who had to be her father, and Wil practically snatched my head off when I spoke to him." She looked from one distraught face to the next.

"I think it's time for a girls' night," Barbara said. "My house, tonight, nine o'clock."

Barbara set a platter of dip surrounded by Wheat Thin crackers, celery sticks and raw baby carrots on the center of her grandmother's table. "The honey-barbecue wings are warming in the oven," she said taking a seat.

"Drink anyone?" Stephanie asked.

Everyone raised their empty glasses. Stephanie poured healthy doses of the frozen apple martinis that Barbara had prepared.

"Who's going first?" Elizabeth said. "'Cause I want to know what I've apparently been missing."

"Since I called this little soiree, I suppose I should," Barbara said. She looked from one to the other. "I slept with Wil," she blurted out before she changed her mind. Although slept wasn't any adequate description.

The shout of "what" was anything but on key.

"You slept with Wil?" Elizabeth croaked in disbelief. "When, where?"

"Today…in the massage room."

Stephanie jumped up. "I knew it, I knew it. I'd recognize that look anywhere," she shouted pointing at Barbara.

Barbara looked mildly embarrassed as her interlude with Wil leaped into her head. "It's not as simple as it sounds."

"Well don't just sit there, spill it," Elizabeth demanded, a bit miffed that Stephanie knew the details before she did.

Barbara brought them all up to date about her earlier relationship with Wil, their breakup and his turning up again after all these years.

"A lot of that going 'round," Ann Marie murmured. "Men just turnin' up like bad pennies." She took a long swallow of her drink.

"Does he know about you and Michael?" Stephanie asked.

"He does now." She told them about her engagement ring falling out of her smock pocket.

"Damn, girl," Ann Marie blurted.

"Let's just say it ended badly," Barbara said.

"What are you going to do?" Elizabeth asked.

"I don't know. I wish I did."

They were all silent, caught up in Barbara's drama.

"What me gone do 'bout Terrance?" Ann Marie asked, breaking the silence.

The trio focused their attention on Ann Marie as she spilled her episode.

"Our lives are anything but boring," Elizabeth muttered.

"You need to come to some decision about Michael first and foremost," Stephanie advised. "How do you feel about him?"

"It's obvious that you still have very strong feelings for Wil," Elizabeth said. "You're not the kind of woman who sleeps around just for the thrill of it."

"Wil doesn't seem to think so," Barbara said, her tone heavy with regret. She looked at her friends. "The last thing I wanted to ever do was hurt him again. Walking away all those years ago was enough."

"He needs to know why," Elizabeth said.

Ann Marie and Stephanie looked at Barbara and nodded in agreement.

Barbara slowly shook her head. "It's probably too late. He'll never speak to me again. And I know he'll never come back to the spa. How am I going to explain?"

Ann Marie cocked her head to the side. "Whatcha think we got that computer for, chile? Look 'im up and go to his house."

"She's right," Stephanie agreed. "You have the information, use it."

"But what about Michael?" Barbara asked.

"You need to search your heart," Elizabeth said. "Only you know how you feel. And if you were able to sleep with Wil…" She let the rest of her telling statement hang in the air.

"Then maybe it's not what you think it is," Stephanie added.

Ann Marie was thoughtful for a moment. Was

what she had with Sterling the real thing or a sub-stitute once again for Terrance?

"Me have the same questions," Ann Marie said softly.

The trio looked in her direction.

"How do you feel about Sterling?" Stephanie asked.

Ann Marie drew in a long breath before speaking. "Been dealing with that question all day."

"And…" Elizabeth asked.

"Sterling is everything I've been looking for. He knows all about Terrance and he still wants to make it work. When I'm with him, nothing else matters."

"I hear a 'but' in there," Elizabeth said.

Ann Marie looked at her. "But when I saw Terrance today…when he kissed me…I was twenty again." She sighed.

"Then you have some decisions to make as well, Ann," Barbara said.

"I know."

"Life is supposed to get easier when you get older," Stephanie groused. "We're all mature women in our forties. We should be enjoying life not embroiled in relationship madness."

"You got that right," Barbara said. "I figured once I hit forty it would be smooth sailing. I'll be fifty in a few months and damn if I don't feel like I'm twenty-one." She chuckled.

"Love is a never ending cycle," Elizabeth said. "As long as we can draw a breath it's going to keep changing and evolving."

"There's got to come a point when all the pieces finally fall into place. I'd hate to be in my seventies bed hopping, if you know what I mean."

"As long as you take your tube of Bengay with you, you'll be fine," Barbara joked.

They all cracked up laughing.

"What's happening with you and Tony anyway?" Elizabeth asked once the laughter had subsided.

"You all will be happy to know that Tony finally convinced me to file a restraining order against Conrad and his crazy-ass wife, Marilyn. And I've seriously been considering what you all suggested before about the sexual harassment suit."

They applauded. Stephanie beamed. "I feel that I can deal with it now. I feel stronger, you know." She looked from one to the other.

Barbara grinned at her. "Love will do that to you—make you strong and weak in the knees at the same time."

"I know that's right," Stephanie said.

They sat back, contemplating their lives while sipping on their drinks. Barbara eased into the silent moment.

"Men may come and go, love can turn to dust, but in the end," she looked from one to the other and raised her glass, "we'll always have each other."

They clicked glasses in a toast.

"To us."

"To success."

"To men!"

"And when all else fails…to great mind-blowing sex!"

"Here, here," they shouted and broke out in fits of laughter.

Chapter 19

Ann Marie was at her desk in the real estate office just finishing up a deal with one of the brokers when Carol, the office assistant, tapped on her door. Ann Marie hung up the phone.

"Yes, come in."

"Ms. Dennis, Terrance Bishop is here to see you."

Ann Marie flinched as a hot flush coursed through her. Her thoughts scrambled.

"Ms. Dennis?"

Ann Marie blinked several times before getting Carol back in focus.

"I can tell him you're busy."

Ann Marie held up her hand. "Just give me a minute. I'll come out."

Carol stared at her for a moment before nodding in agreement. She stepped out and shut the door behind her.

Ann Marie pushed her fist to her mouth. She wasn't ready to see Terrance again so soon. *You have to deal with it*, she heard her friends saying in her head. She wished they were standing beside her now.

Pushing herself up from her seat, she tugged down on the hem of her deep burgundy Valentino jacket and brushed her hands down the sides of the matching skirt. "Now or never," she murmured. She walked to the door, opened it and stepped out into the front foyer. She spotted him seated in the guest lounge through the glass doors. If only she could forever seal him inside and move on with her life. Wishful thinking. Now or never.

She crossed the short hall and opened the door to the lounge. Terrance turned, the smile that had melted the hearts of many moved easily across his handsome face. He put down the magazine he'd held in his hands.

"I'd hoped you would decide to see me. Sorry to show up at your place of business." He looked around, appraising the space. "You've done well for yourself, Mari."

Ann Marie walked fully into the room. "What do you want, Terrance? You've already charmed your daughter."

He took a step toward her. "I want to talk with you."

"I'm very busy."

"I wanted to let you know that I'm heading back home in a couple of days. I want you to come back with me."

Her stomach somersaulted. "Forget it." She shook her head. "I'm not going back."

"Have you no good memories of home, of us?" He stepped closer. She drew in a breath as his scent wafted to her nose.

"That was a long time ago."

"I haven't forgotten."

She turned her head away. "Maybe it's time you did."

"Never."

There was that word again.

"I want a divorce, Terrance." For an instant he seemed to shrink before pulling himself together. She lifted her chin in defiance. "That's all I want from you."

He pursed his lips in thought. "I'll make you a deal."

Her brow rose with suspicion. "What kind of deal?"

"You come back with me to Jamaica. Give me two weeks. If at the end of the two weeks you still feel the same way, I'll give you your divorce." He watched her expression process the information. "Besides, if you don't come, I will have no choice but to fight it and then you will have to come home to settle it all anyway."

Fury singed her cheeks. "So you've stooped to blackmail," she said walking up on him. "Is nothing beneath you?"

"I will do whatever is necessary to have what I what. If you remember nothing else about me, remember that. And I want you."

She spun away, folded her arms beneath her pert breasts as she paced. Her thoughts raced in a million directions at once. He had her up against the wall, just where he wanted her. Her options were minimal. She stopped, dropped her hands to her sides.

"I'll give you your two weeks Terrance and then I want my divorce."

The corner of his mouth curved upward. "You made the right decision, Mari, and I guarantee," he stepped up to her and lifted her chin with the tip of his finger, "two weeks back together and all notions of divorce will be a distant memory." His eyes bored into hers. She held her breath then jerked away.

"Leave."

He reached into his pocket and pulled out an envelope then tossed it onto the desk. "Your ticket is inside." He turned and walked out.

On wobbly legs she walked to her desk and picked up the envelope. Just as he said, a ticket to Jamaica, first class was inside—*one way*. She glanced toward the door. Arrogant, self-assured, sexy bastard!

She slowly sat down. How was she going to explain this to Sterling?

Chapter 20

Barbara fingered her engagement ring as she paced her apartment. She checked the clock for the third time in the past half hour. Michael would be arriving any minute.

As usual his impromptu visit was a surprise. He was only scheduled to be in town for two days during a short training break. The season was set to start in two weeks and he was back on the roster. Every newspaper that she picked up had the story of point guard Michael Townsend's return and with his return, hopes for an NBA championship for his team.

When Michael came into her life, and she finally allowed her heart to open and let him in, she was certain that he would be the last stop for her. Since her husband Marvin's death years earlier, Barbara had put love on the back burner. Michael came along and reignited the pilot. But his youth had always nagged at her as much as he and her friends insisted that it didn't matter. Soon she would be fifty. Michael was in his early thirties. He'd want children at some point. Something she could not give him, something she had not discussed with him. And then there was Wil. William Hutchinson, her first love, her soulmate, the man she'd run from, was back and everything that she thought was solid in her life was crumbling into little pieces. She still loved him, never stopped. So what did that mean about her feelings for Michael? Is it possible to love two people at the same time? And if she was truly in love with Michael would she have been able to make love so passionately with Wil?

What did that dilemma matter? Wil didn't want to have anything to do with her. She couldn't blame him. By omission she'd deceived him— again. But was she willing to compound her transgression by going on as usual with Michael?

These were the questions, along with countless

others, that had plagued her since she regained her senses in the massage room. God, what must Wil think of her?

She jumped at the sound of the doorbell. *Michael.* Her pulse raced. She brushed back her hair and walked to the front door. Smoothing her expression, she pulled the door open.

Michael's handsome face grinned at her.

"Hey baby." He crossed the threshold and took her in his arms for a long kiss. "I missed you," he murmured against her mouth before reluctantly letting her go.

She stroked his face and looked into his dark eyes, remembering all the reasons why she'd said yes to his proposal of marriage. "Missed you, too." She took his hand. "Come in." She pushed the door shut behind him.

"It sure feels good to be back." He turned to her. "Especially seeing you. Seems like forever."

"How was your flight?" she asked, sidestepping his comments.

"Not bad. Usual hassles." He lowered himself onto the couch and stretched his hand out to her. She crossed the room and sat next to him. He draped his long arm around her shoulders and pulled her closer. "So what have you been up to?"

"Keeping busy that's for sure. We did finally

hire a few new people so that has taken off some of the load."

"Great. That will make more time for us. Next time I ask you to come visit you won't have any reason to say no."

Although his comment was simple enough, his sarcastic tone rubbed Barbara the wrong way.

She eased out of his hold and turned to his profile. "You make it sound as though I was making up an excuse not to come out to Florida."

He rocked his jaw a moment then looked her in the eye. "It's not about excuses, it's about you being my woman, my fiancée, my soon-to-be wife and being there for me."

Her neck jerked back. "What are you saying? That my life is not as important as yours?"

His thick brows drew together. "Let's be for real. I make two million plus per year, after taxes. If I don't play another game in my life I'm still set. I could buy that spa right out from under you. What you do has its merits...but come on."

She couldn't believe what she was hearing. She jumped up from her seat and glared down at him, her finger pointing at his face. "You play a *game* for a living. A game! I do something meaning-ful—I *help* people. And let's not forget I helped your two-million-plus-per-year-after-taxes ass!"

He held up his hands. "Barbara, chill. I didn't mean it like that. You're—"

"You didn't?" She tossed her head back and laughed a nasty laugh. "Oh, I see, you didn't mean to insult me and what I do for a living. Is that what you're telling me? Pardon me for the confusion." She spun away and stormed off to her bedroom, slamming the door behind her.

She paced her bedroom, arms folded, fury boiled inside her pounding against her temples. How dare he? How dare he undermine her that way? Is that what he really thought? What had she gotten herself into?

A tentative knock halted her parade in mid-step.

"I'm coming in." Michael opened the door. "I'm sorry. It was stupid and insensitive." He walked into the room after offering his olive branch. "Sometimes I talk faster than I think." He approached her. She stiffened. "You have to know I wouldn't do anything to hurt you. I'm sorry," he repeated.

Barbara loosened the hold she had on herself and looked up at him—seeing all the things she'd always seen but refused to believe. Michael Townsend was still a young man in so many ways. And his celebrity and his money camouflaged his immaturity. There'd been all the signs, his moodiness, pouting when things didn't go his way, his irrational possessiveness, not to mention the 'baby mama drama' scare. Sure he was an incredible lover, kind, gentle and fun to be with. But she needed more than that. She needed someone on her level, someone who both understood and respected her totally. She didn't have enough good years left to 'train' anyone. They had to come ready to play. She let out a breath.

"Mike, sit down...please."

He did as she asked, sitting on the side of her bed.

"When you came into my life, everything in it changed, including me—all for the better." She smiled softly. "But we are much too different, Mike, and it's not just the age, although that's a big part of it. I can't run every time you say how fast, nor do I want to. You'd love a great piece of eye-candy for your arm when you are out in public and let's be for real—I ain't the one. As much as you say otherwise." She paused a moment. "And what about a family, Michael? I—"

"That's not important."

"You say that now. But it will be and it's not fair to deprive you of that." She glanced down at her folded hands and slipped the ring from her finger. She handed it to him.

He shook his head. "Don't do this."

"It's the right thing to do." Her voice broke.

"You brightened my world, you gave me love when I didn't think it would come my way again. For that I will always be grateful, and I will always love you for it. But…this won't work between us."

Michael drew in a long, shaky breath. "You keep the ring." He stood and looked down at her. "I don't ever want you to forget that you were and always will be loved by me." He leaned down and tenderly kissed her forehead. "Be happy." He turned and walked out.

Barbara hugged her arms tightly to her body and rocked back and forth on the bed. She wanted to go after him, tell him she was just afraid, that what she said was a mistake and that she was sorry. That wasn't the answer. She knew it wasn't. As much as it was tearing her apart inside to know that she'd hurt him, she knew she did the right thing.

Tears of acceptance slid down her cheeks. She was back where she started. She turned the ring around in her palm, the light dancing off the perfect stone. Hopefully, she was a little wiser.

Chapter 21

"I'm glad you made this decision to take out the restraining order, Steph," Tony said as they pulled out from in front of her apartment building. "Now both Conrad and his wife will know that you mean business." He stole a glance at her somber expression. "Are you okay?"

"Yeah, I'm good. I wish it wouldn't have come to this. I feel so stupid."

"Don't. We all make mistakes."

"This was major." She stared out the window. "Do you regret telling me?"

She turned her head in his direction. "At

first…yes…I wasn't sure how you were going to take it, what you were going to think of me."

"And now?"

"I'm glad I did. It showed me the kind of man you really are."

"And that's a good thing?" He winked.

"Definitely." She squeezed his thigh.

"After this court thing what do you have planned for the rest of the day?"

"Hmm, I have a late afternoon meeting with Terri Wells the PR rep from Sterns & Blac."

"Oh yeah, about the Pause Man." He chuckled, dragging out the two words.

She gave him a playful sock in the arm. "What's so funny?"

"Nothing, seriously. I always think of women in these kinds of competitions. Guess it's the old-school guy in me."

"You should apply. You'd make a great spokes-man, not to mention the prizes."

He vigorously shook his head. "Oh no, not me. I'm definitely not the one. I prefer to be behind the camera, not in front of it."

"Coward."

"Oh…so soon we've resorted to name-calling. What next?"

Stephanie shook her head and laughed. "You are too silly."

He pulled up to the light and looked at her with a devilish gleam in his eyes. "But you love me, anyway."

The L word. Her chest tightened. She knew she cared deeply for Tony. He was everything she could possibly want in a man and he cared about her for who she was, warts and all. Love? He was kidding—of course. She smiled. "Who wouldn't?"

His expression seemed to flutter before her eyes as if he'd been surprised by a pinprick. "Exactly. Who wouldn't?" he finally said, his tone missing its earlier lightness.

Stephanie ran her tongue across her lips and directed all her attention on the traffic ahead, as if she could move the stalled line of cars with her mind.

She'd made a mess of her love life, long before the fiasco with her former boss, Conrad. Much of it had to do with her own lack of esteem and, of course, the guilt about her sister Samantha. There was a part of her that believed she wasn't truly deserving of love and happiness. As a result she continually found men who didn't have her best interests at heart, got involved in relationships that she knew could go nowhere, even as she tried to convince herself otherwise.

Now Tony was in her life and he had no qualms about proving to her that he was for real and wanted to be a permanent part of her life. Was she mentally and emotionally ready for what Tony was offering?

The car drew to a stop. Stephanie blinked. She'd totally zoned out. They were in front of the courthouse.

"Here we are. Do you want me to come in with you?"

"No. I need to do this myself." She leaned over and cupped his chin in her palm. Gently she kissed his lips then eased back. "Thank you…for everything."

"For you—anything."

"I still want you to come meet my sister this evening."

"Of course." He smiled gently. "I'm looking forward to it. I know it's not a decision you came to easily. I appreciate you trusting me enough to let me into such a private part of your life."

She lowered her gaze. "In all my adult life…since the accident, no one has met Samantha."

Tony's brow wrinkled in concern. "What about your parents, Steph? You never talk about them."

She tugged on her bottom lip with her teeth. Her

parents. That was a joke. "My father has been missing in action since Sam and I were toddlers. He could be sitting right next to me and I wouldn't know him." She drew in a breath of pain. "My mom was never really there for us growing up. She was too busy looking for Mr. Right Now. After the accident she totally gave up on us. Came to see Sam one day at the hospital," her voice cracked, "and never came back. I've been taking care of her ever since."

Tony grabbed her hand. "I'm sorry. I didn't mean to open old wounds."

She shook her head. "It's all right. I never talk about it." She looked into his eyes. "Maybe it's time that I do."

"Whenever you're ready, I'm here."

She swallowed over the tight knot in her throat and nodded her head. "Well, I better get in there." She sniffed and blinked back the tears that threatened to fall. "I understand it can be a long process." She forced a smile.

Tony's eyes explored her face. "You're going to be okay. Believe that."

"I'm working on it." She unfastened her seatbelt, opened the door and hopped out of the Navigator. She peered into the window. "See you later.

Good luck with the photo shoot." He was doing a spread for a corporate brochure that morning.

"Piece of cake. I'll see you back at your place around six."

"Okay." She waved and walked toward the steps of the court.

Tony watched her from the window. There was so much about Stephanie that he knew and so much that he didn't. He wanted to be there for her every step of the way, if she would only let him. She pushed through the revolving doors and merged with the crowd. Tony put the SUV in gear and slowly drove off. Today was a major step for them both. Hopefully they would take many more steps together.

Ann Marie left the office early and went straight home. She needed to talk to Sterling. She thought of the airline ticket burning a hole in her pocketbook and fretted about how she would find the words to explain what she needed to do to Sterling. It was a lot for anyone to swallow but she didn't see any other way around it. She wanted her divorce and if it took going back to Jamaica and dealing with Terrance for two weeks then so be it.

She flipped on the lights in the apartment then went to her bedroom. Sitting on the edge of her bed, she picked up the phone from the nightstand

and dialed Sterling's number before she lost her nerve. He answered on the third ring.

"Hey, sweetie. This is a pleasant surprise." He closed the folder on his desk and leaned back in his leather swivel chair.

"I was hoping I could see you later."

"Do you need to ask?" He chuckled. "You want to come by my place?"

"Um, I was thinking that I'd fix dinner and we could relax over here." She felt more in control in her own surroundings.

"Not a problem. Need me to bring anything?"

"Uh, no. I'm sure I have everything I need."

He paused a moment. "Is everything okay with you? You sound funny."

She cleared her throat. "I'm fine. Just a hectic day at work, that's all."

"Hey, listen we can go out so you won't have to trouble yourself fixing anything if you're tired."

"No. It's okay. I want to."

"Well…if you're sure."

"I'm sure." She really wasn't sure about anything. "So how about nine?"

"No problem. Gives me time to finish up here and dart home for a few minutes. I'll see you at nine."

"Bye."

"For now."

Ann Marie blew out a shaky breath and hung up the phone. The first hurdle was out of the way, but the big one was yet to come.

She got up from the bed and went into the bathroom for a quick shower. All the while she thought about maybe just getting him drunk and telling him that way.

As the hour drew near, Ann Marie began to doubt the veracity of her plan. Maybe there was some way she could get what she wanted without giving into Terrance's demands. Good idea, but she didn't see how she could make it work. If nothing else, Terrance Bishop was good as his word. He would make her life hell. And she had plans to spend the rest of her days in someplace other than there.

The alarm on the oven went off. Her broiled salmon was ready. She took the tray out of the oven and put it on the side counter. She checked the saffron rice with peas and turned that off as well. The chef salad was in the fridge. Ordinarily she would have cooked up a feast, but she wanted to keep it simple. Besides, she didn't have the concentration for much else.

She took two plates from the glass cabinet and put them on the dining table, flatware from the drawer and two glasses from the cabinet. Just as she was fixing the place settings the bell rang. For a moment she squeezed her eyes shut and said a silent prayer that the evening wouldn't turn out as ugly as she imagined.

Wiping her hands on a red and white dishtowel she went to the door and opened it.

Her expectant expression froze along with her body. The last person she expected to see was Raquel.

"I know you weren't expecting me and I shouldn't have come without calling." She fidgeted with her purse. "But I wanted to talk to you—to apologize."

Ann Marie exhaled in relief. The strain between them for the last month had taken more of a toll on her than she was willing to admit.

"Do you want to come in or stand 'ere and speak our business in the street?"

Raquel pressed her lips together and walked inside. "Thank you," she murmured.

Ann Marie closed the door softly behind her then followed her inside.

Raquel took a seat on the lounge chair. Ann Marie sat opposite her on the couch. For several moments an uncomfortable silence took up the space between them.

Raquel cleared her throat. "I…I'm sorry for the way I acted and the things I said to you. I had no right to judge you." She looked into her mother's eyes. "I was angry and confused. I never gave you a chance to tell your side. That was unfair of me."

"Thank you for that. It takes a lot to say sorry." She paused trying to find the right words to explain the unexplainable to her daughter. "I should have told you the whole story about me and your dad years ago or at least when you were old enough to understand."

"Why didn't you?"

Ann Marie sighed, looked off into the distance then focused back on Raquel. "I was ashamed."

"Ashamed? Why?"

"Of being such a weak woman. Of letting a man have such control over my happiness. Of sitting by and allowing him to run his life as he chose without any regard for me." She looked at her daughter and saw Terrance and for the first time it was all right. "I never wanted you to see me as weak. I didn't want that to be the image of what you thought a woman should be."

"Sometimes love does make you weak." She thought of her own failed marriage to Earl and inwardly cringed. "But it doesn't have to make you bitter." She drew in a breath. "What hurt me the most,

Mama, was not having a father it was not having you. Everyday I blamed myself for your lack of love for me. And I didn't know what to do to fix it."

"I'd hardened my heart Raquel. Hardened it to anything good. I cut my feelings off. Too scared to care about anyone that much again. In my mind, love equaled pain and betrayal."

"It doesn't have to. Only if you let it."

"I know that now. Because of you and…because of Sterling." She sat back and a slow smile curved her mouth. She told Raquel that her return into her life had opened her up again and as a result she knew she was capable of love and worthy of receiving it as well as giving it. Then she went on to tell her about Terrance's proposition.

"So what are you going to do?"

"I don't have much of a choice. I was planning on telling Sterling tonight. He should be here any minute."

Raquel jumped up. "I should go."

"No." Ann Marie held up her hand. "Stay."

"I think it's best that you deal with this without me."

Ann Marie flashed a crooked smile. "I was hoping you could stick around for moral support."

"You're a big woman," Raquel teased in a perfect Jamaican lilt. "You'll be fine." She fished in her purse and wrote something down on a piece of paper then handed it to her mother. "In case you want to talk."

Ann Marie looked at the paper. It was Raquel's number at the hotel where she was staying. A knot of guilt formed in the center of her chest. "Why don't you come back here?"

Raquel shook her head. "One hard lesson you taught me was to stand on my own two feet. I have a good job and I'll be moving into my own place in a couple of weeks. I purchased a condo in lower Manhattan. I'll be a home owner for the first time." She smiled brightly.

"That's wonderful!" She sobered and took Raquel's cheeks in her hands. "I've never told you how proud I am of you."

"I needed to hear that."

Ann Marie placed a gentle kiss on her cheek.

Raquel stepped back, her gaze soft. "I'll call you."

Ann Marie could only nod her head, afraid that if she spoke she'd burst into uncharacteristic tears.

Raquel turned and left. Thoughtfully, Ann Marie closed the door. For all the mother that she'd never been to Raquel, she'd turned out to be a fine woman in spite of it.

Before she'd gotten halfway back into the house, the bell rang again. This time it was Sterling.

"Hey beautiful." He kissed her long and slow.

"Hey yourself," she breathed against his mouth. "Come on in. Dinner's ready."

"Smells delicious."

"Want a glass of wine first or something stronger?"

"No. I'm good."

"I thought we could eat in the dining room."

"Rather formal tonight, aren't we?" He gave her a curious look.

She averted her gaze. "Not at all." She led him into the dining room then began fixing their plates.

"Something is bothering you." He stepped up beside her. She focused on what she was doing. "Would you look at me?"

"Hmm." She gave him a millisecond of eye contact. "What?"

"What is going on with you? You're not acting like yourself."

She slid a piece of salmon onto his plate and forced a smile. "Who me actin' like?"

He clasped her shoulder and turned her around. "That's what I'm trying to find out."

She eased out of his grasp. "Let's sit down. I need to talk."

She sat at the table in the kitchen. Sterling pulled up a seat. He folded his hands on top of the table. "I'm listening."

"I have to go to Jamaica."

He frowned in confusion. "What are you talking about? Why?"

She swallowed. "To get my divorce."

He was silent for a moment, processing the information. He zeroed in on her. "When did you come to this realization?"

Tell him. Tell him. "Terrance is here. He said if I came back to Jamaica, he would give me my divorce."

Sterling's face contorted into a series of hard lines. "I see. And when were you going to tell me that your *husband* was in town?"

"He only just arrived. He's leaving day after tomorrow...and he wants me to go with him."

Sterling stood. "Really?" He crossed the room in two long strides then swung around to confront her half-baked story. "What else does he want, Ann?"

She felt hot all over. "Me," she whispered.

He expelled a nasty chuckle. "Figures. And you're just playing along I take it."

"If there was any other way I would do it!"

"Would you?" He approached her. "There's still something between the two of you. It's obvious every time you mention the man's name and you can barely look at me when you do. And now you're going to run off to some island with him?"

He tossed his head back and laughed devoid of any humor. "That's rich. That's real rich." He glared at her. "And tell me *Mrs*. Bishop what the hell am I supposed to be doing while you work things out with *Mr*. Bishop?"

Ann Marie's nostrils flared as she sucked in air. She pushed up from the table, her palms pressed down on the surface, her accent getting the best of her. "T'ink what ya wan'. Me g'wan do this t'ing or me never be free of 'im. Don't you understand that?"

"I don't understand much of anything when it comes to you Ann Marie. Not much of anything. Do what you need to do. But I wouldn't bet money that I'll be waiting when you get back." He shoved the chair under the table and stormed out.

She lowered herself back into the chair. The sound of her front door slamming ricocheted around in her head.

Yep, it was just as bad as she'd imagined.

Chapter 22

"Ready?" Stephanie asked Tony as they walked down the corridor of the facility.

He took her hand. "Absolutely." He kissed her lightly on the cheek.

"She's in the room down this hallway. Don't get upset when you see her. She doesn't react well to strangers." She babbled to cover up her jangling nerves.

"Babe, relax. It's going to be fine."

She looked at him and flashed a tight smile then stopped in front of Samantha's door. She knocked and slowly opened the door. Sam was seated as always in her favorite place by the window. Stephanie approached slowly. She knelt down in front of her sister.

"Sam. Hey sweetie." She took her chin and forced Samantha to focus on her. "It's me, Stephanie. How are you today?" She brushed the hair away from her face.

For a moment Samantha focused on her sister. Light brightened her usually vacant gaze. "Steph…anie," she slurred.

Stephanie's heart lurched, a smile blooming across her face. She looked up at Tony and stretched her hand out to him. "I want you to meet a friend of mine. His name is Tony."

Tony stepped into Samantha's line of sight. For a moment he was speechless. They were identical. Except for the eyes. Where Stephanie's brown eyes held fire and light and passion, Samantha's were almost empty, devoid of life. "Hi, Sam. Your sister has told me all about you."

Samantha looked at him for a moment then slowly the light faded and she turned her face away.

Stephanie gave Tony an apologetic look.

"I'll wait outside," he mouthed. Stephanie nodded her head. Once Tony was gone, Stephanie turned her attention back to her sister.

"The doctors say you're doing so much better,

sweetie. That's such good news." She held Samantha's hands as she spoke. "They are going to start you back on speech therapy again. Would you like that?"

Samantha sighed heavily. She pointed to the window. "Out...side."

Stephanie blinked back her surprise. "You want to go outside? Is that what you're telling me?"

"Out...side," she repeated, like an infant testing the language.

Stephanie drew in a shaky breath. "Okay." She took Samantha's hand and helped her to her feet. "Let's go outside." She led her out of the room and down the hallway.

"Where are you going?" one of the nurses asked, stopping her in the hall.

"I'm going to take her for a short walk on the grounds." Stephanie smiled brightly then looked at her sister. "She asked me to."

"I'll get someone to go with you."

Samantha suddenly shook her head wildly.

"Okay, sweetie, relax. It will be just you and me. Just us." She pleaded to the nurse with her eyes.

"Just on the grounds," the nurse warned. "And she needs a coat."

Stephanie nodded her head, took off her suede jacket and put it around Samantha's shoulders.

She hooked Samantha's arm through hers and led her down the hallway toward the door that opened to the grounds in back.

Tony saw them and got up from the bench where he'd been seated in the waiting area. Stephanie subtly waved him off and walked outside.

"It's a beautiful day for fall," Stephanie said as the first bite of chill hit them. "Are you warm enough?" Sam kept walking, looking around as if seeing the world for the first time.

She stood in the center of the courtyard and turned in a slow circle. The muffled sounds of traffic could be heard in the background. She faced her sister and smiled a real smile. Stephanie's hand flew to her mouth.

"Chilly," Sam murmured and grinned, hugging the jacket around her.

"Yes, it's chilly." Stephanie ran her hands up and down her arms, thankful for her sweater. "In a couple of months it will be Christmas and there will be snow."

"Snow." She grinned again. She walked toward the bench beneath a naked tree and sat down. Stephanie joined her and put her arm around her shoulders.

Sam rested her head against Stephanie's neck. "Tony?"

Stephanie angled her head to look at Sam. "You want to know about Tony?"

"Tony?" she repeated.

Stephanie slowly told Samantha how they'd met and how important he'd become to her.

"I care about him a lot," she concluded. "I hope you'll like him too."

Sam was quiet for a long while. "Cold," she finally said.

"Okay, let's go back inside."

They got up and walked hand-in-hand back inside.

"I still can't believe it," Stephanie said, once she and Tony were in the car. "It's been years. The doctors had totally given up on her ever speaking or even thinking clearly again." She turned in her seat. "This is the first time in over a decade that my sister has spoken to me." Her voice crumbled into little pieces. "You have no idea how that feels." Tears spilled over her lashes.

Tony squeezed her thigh. "I can only imagine," he said softly.

"I know it's too much to hope for but maybe one day she will actually get out of here."

"Will you stop feeling guilty then, if she does?"

Stephanie lowered her head. "I don't know if

that will ever happen," she confessed. "If it wasn't for me, she wouldn't be here. I don't see how I can ever forgive myself for that."

"But maybe *she* has."

"Dad, you want to tell me what's buggin' you?" Chauncey asked, taking a seat opposite his father at the kitchen table.

"Don't you have homework to do or something?"

"No. All done." He studied his father's dour expression. "Something's got you bummed out. Is it work?"

"No. Work is fine. Look I really don't want to talk about it right now."

"Maybe you should go down to the spa and work off some of the stress that's written all over your face."

Wil suddenly pushed up from the table. "That's not gonna happen."

"Why not? I thought you liked it."

"Forget it! Okay." He stormed out of the kitchen and into his bedroom, shutting the door behind him.

He tossed his house keys on top of the dresser. He shouldn't have barked at Chauncey that way. It wasn't his fault that Barbara had screwed him over for a second time.

Engaged! Every time he thought about it and

thought about how they felt so right together he wanted to hit something—hard. How could she do something like that? What kind of woman had she turned out to be? Or maybe she hadn't turned out any different from the girl he knew in college. He snorted in disgust. He'd been a fool for her back then and he was still a fool.

He heard the front doorbell ring. *Probably one of Chauncey's friends.* Good that would keep him out of his hair for a few hours. He took off his shirt and tossed it on the bed. Maybe an ice-cold beer and a hot shower would make him feel halfway human again. He walked into the master bath adjoining his room, thankful for that bit of privacy. Just as he was about to turn on the shower he heard a knock on his door.

"Be back here before eleven. It's a school night," he shouted.

Chauncey cracked the door open. "Dad. Someone's here to see you."

Wil turned, his expression still tight. "Who?"

"The lady from the spa. Ms. Allen," he said in a hushed tone.

Wil blinked. "What?"

"The lady from the spa. She said she wants to talk to you."

"Tell her I've canceled my membership."

"What did you go and do that for?"

"Tell her what I said!"

Chauncey huffed and walked away. Several moments later he was back. "She said she's not leaving until you speak to her. Is something going on with you two?"

Wil stalked over to his bed, snatched up his shirt and put it on. He wagged a warning finger. "That's none of your business." He came to the door and pushed passed his son. "Go find something to do in your room for a few minutes, will ya?"

Chauncey grinned. "Sure, Dad."

Wil walked into the kitchen. Barbara had her back to him.

"What are you doing here?"

She swung toward him, something akin to fear in her eyes. "I wanted to talk to you, Wil." She twisted her hands in front of her.

"What do you want to tell me this time? Oh, that's right, you don't generally tell me anything—shit just happens." He crossed the room, snatched open the fridge and took out a beer. He didn't offer her one.

"You have every right to be angry," she began.

He glared at her. "Ya think?"

Barbara flinched but was determined to do what she'd come there to do. "I'm sorry. About everything, not just the other day."

"Yeah, me too, Barbara." He looked into her eyes and for a moment his heart softened when he saw the pleading in hers. "Have a seat," he said grudgingly.

Tentatively she sat down, thankful to get off her trembling legs. She folded her hands on top of the table to keep them from shaking. "There's so much you need to know."

He took a long swallow of his beer but didn't respond.

"Back when we were in college…"

She told him about finding out that she was pregnant, her fear, her joy mixed with sadness and what it would ultimately do to his life.

"I was so confused. I didn't know where to turn."

He was trying to process the information. Barbara had been pregnant with his child? Emotions that he couldn't give a name to ran rampant through his insides. He looked into her eyes. "You could have turned to me."

She shook her head. "I know what you would have said, and I would have agreed and any chance you had to play professional ball would have been over. I couldn't do that to you."

"So you killed our child instead." Fury burned his gut.

"No!" she cried. "No. I didn't."

He frowned in confusion. "Then what happened?"

She told him of her trip to New York, of her clinic visit and ultimately her decision to keep their child, and then the miscarriage.

Wil squeezed his eyes shut as he imagined the woman he loved alone and terrified. His hand stretched across the table, bridging the great divide that had separated them for so long.

Barbara took his hand and finished her story, including the painful visit at the hospital by her mother.

"I don't know what to say," Wil murmured.

Barbara inhaled deeply. "About the other day..."

Wil's features tightened. He looked away then slowly got up from the table, turning his back to her.

"I wasn't thinking," she started. "The only thing that was clear to me was that you were back in my life and that even after everything, even after convincing myself that I could marry again, all I knew at that moment was that I was still in love with you. That I'd never stopped loving you."

Tentatively he turned around and when he looked at her all the years peeled away. He couldn't speak. How many years had he longed to hear those words? How many pointless relationships had he gone through hoping to recapture what they'd once shared together?

"Well…that's all I came to say." She took up her purse from the table and stood up. "Maybe one day you can forgive me." She started for the door, opened it and walked out.

Wil collapsed into the chair, staring at the closed door. It was all too much to process. Did she think that simply confessing her undying love would somehow magically erase all the pain he'd lived with for so long? If only life was that simple.

"Dad?" Chauncey eased into the room.

Wil kept his back to him, unwilling to let his son see the tears in his eyes. He sniffed and headed for the fridge. He took out another beer, while pulling himself together.

"Everything okay?"

"Fine."

Chauncey watched his father's stiff back before returning to his room.

"Everything is just fine," he murmured and took a slow swallow of his beer.

Chapter 23

Ann Marie checked her two suitcases at the ticket counter then looked around the terminal for the departure gate. She had yet to spot Terrance who'd said he'd meet her.

More than once she'd considered changing her mind, especially after the way Sterling reacted. Her doubts had grown so worrisome that she'd actually called Stephanie to talk it over. Stephanie told her to do what was in her heart and if she and Sterling were meant to be, he'd be waiting when she returned. Ann Marie agreed. She needed to hear it from someone else. This was the only way.

If there was any chance for her to make a life with Sterling she must get her freedom and put Terrance behind her once and for all. When she returned a free woman, she'd find a way to make it all up to Sterling.

She followed the long line of travelers toward the security gates and passed through without incident. She adjusted her oversize bag on her shoulder and headed for her departure gate. She looked around for an empty seat and found one near the window. She set her bag down at her feet and settled back to wait. There was at least another half hour before boarding. She pulled out a magazine from her bag.

"Here you are."

Ann Marie's pulse quickened. She looked up. Terrance took a seat next to her. "I wasn't sure if you would come."

"I told you I would. I want my divorce."

He merely smiled. "I always wondered how you could have stayed away from home for so long."

"No reason to return."

"Was it that bad, Mari?"

She flipped open the magazine and tried to concentrate on the words, ignoring his question.

"This can be a pleasant trip, if you let it."

She snatched a look at him then turned back to her magazine.

Shortly after, the flight was announced and much to Ann Marie's dismay, she was seated next to Terrance for the entire trip.

He tried to make small talk at first until she feigned exhaustion and shut her eyes. But that didn't stop her heart from racing like crazy with the thought of him next to her, so close for so many hours. She forced her mind to drift—any place but on thoughts of Terrance. But the mind is a funny animal. The smooth motion of the plane, the days of tension finally took its toll and she was slowly lulled into the cocoon of sleep.

She was an innocent teen, slender with hair down to the middle of her back. She was frolicking along the beach, darting in and out of the waves. She was to be married the following afternoon to a man she loved with all her heart. Terrance Bishop was handsome, wealthy and she knew many women in her Parrish wished they were in her shoes.

Her story was one from a fairytale. A Cinderella tale. She'd come to the Bishop household practically a servant and ended up engaged to one of the most eligible bachelors in all of Jamaica.

Terrance, at first, was a total gentleman, keeping his distance, speaking to her casually when he ran into her in the house or out on the grounds. Every time she saw him, her stomach and her heart would do funny things inside of her. She tried to keep her mind off him by working hard and swimming. One of her little secrets was a little cove that she'd discovered while walking along the grounds of the Bishop household. It was tucked away near the shore but out of sight of the main house.

One afternoon, she emerged from a swim exhilarated, dripping wet and in search of her towel. She was certain she'd left it on top of the small rock formation. Her clothes were gone, too.

"Looking for these?"

She spun toward the voice, crisscrossing her arms over her body to shield her nakedness. She wanted to die.

"I was strolling along and saw the clothes." He stepped closer. "I couldn't imagine who would have left their clothes out here."

She felt paralyzed.

"You're much too beautiful to cover yourself up." He walked right to her. Only the bundle of clothes separated them. First he pushed aside the wet locks of hair plastered to the sides of her face. Then he removed her hands from her body one by one. He stepped back. His dark eyes burned up and down her flesh, seeming to make the water sizzle on her skin.

He gave her the clothing and without another word turned and walked away.

She was mortified. How would she ever be able to go back to work in the Bishop household after Terrance had seen her naked? What was she going to do? Her mother would never let her return home.

But she didn't have to worry about it. By the time she reached the main house, Terrance was sitting out on the porch, drinking an ice-cold glass of *mauby.* He smiled as she approached.

"No reason to hang your head."

She dared to look up at him as she took the first step.

"Why don't you join me?" He extended his hand toward the empty seat on the opposite side of the white wood table.

Ann Marie looked around in a panic. How would it look if she were seen lounging on the front porch with the man of the house?

"Don't worry," he'd said, as if reading her mind. "No one would dare say a word." Tentatively she sat down.

Terrance poured her a glass of *mauby* and then began talking with her as if they were old friends. Before she knew it the sun had begun to set over the ocean.

"Be ready tomorrow evening around eight. I want to take you sailing. Wear something pretty."

And that's how it began. From that day forward she was Terrance's woman and less than a year later they were married.

A series of bumps rocked her from sleep. She blinked then jerked up, realizing not only had they landed but she'd fallen asleep on Terrance's shoulder with his arm wrapped around her.

"You were resting so comfortably I didn't want to disturb you. Thought I'd let you rest until we arrived." He grinned at her. "You still snore in your sleep."

She made a face. "Do not."

"That's what you always say." He unfastened his seatbelt.

The familiarity that ebbed and flowed between them was unnerving. The sooner they got this farce over with, the happier she would be. And why in hell did it have to feel so right waking up in his arms?

They disembarked from the plane and wound their way around the throngs of tourists and native islanders. The instant she stepped out into the brilliant sunshine and inhaled the salty sweet air, a pang of longing went off inside her. She didn't realize how much she missed home until that moment. The sky was a brilliant blue, palms swayed in the sea-drunk breeze, the familiar rapid-fire tongues of the native Jamaicans rang like music in her ears. The streets teamed with vendors and shoppers and cars drove on the left side of the street.

Home. It felt so good to be back she wanted to cry with joy, but she wouldn't give Terrance the satisfaction.

A limo driver approached and took Terrance's bag and then Ann Marie's. "Good trip, sir?"

"Great, Marshall. Mrs. Bishop has two more suitcases."

Marshall bowed. "Good to see you again, Mrs. Bishop." He smiled in recognition.

Ann Marie was so surprised at seeing Marshall again she was momentarily at a loss for words. Being called Mrs. Bishop twice in matter of seconds didn't help. Finally she found her voice. "Good to see you too, Marshall."

Terrance strode toward the waiting car, holding tight to Ann Marie's hand.

"I'm not going to run off, Terrance. You don't have to latch on to me."

He brought her hand to his lips and kissed it. "I don't want to take any chances."

Marshall hurried forward and opened the doors. Terrance helped Ann Marie inside.

"Is it what you remember?" he asked as they drove from the airport, through the main part of town then out to the country.

Ann Marie had been staring out of the window for most of the trip, her nose pressed against the glass, like a small child watching their first snowfall.

"Yes," she answered wistfully. "It does. A lot more building going on since I've left."

"Yes, we do try to keep up with the rest of the world," he joked.

The car slowed to a halt and Ann Marie's heart caught in her throat. They were in front of the Bishop estate, the very place where she'd fallen in love with him, became his wife, the lady of the house, slept with him, bore his child. The house she'd loved and left behind.

Marshall was standing there with the door open. She couldn't move.

"Mrs.?"

Ann Marie blinked. "Oh, I'm sorry." She accepted his hand and alighted from the car. Terrance stepped out behind her.

He leaned down near her ear. "Welcome home, Mari."

A shudder shimmied through her. She turned, looked up at him. "I'd rather stay in a hotel."

He pressed his palm against the small of her back. Heat scorched the spot. "Don't be silly. This house is big enough for both of us." He guided her inside.

As she crossed the threshold, she thoroughly doubted that statement.

Marshall led her up the stairs. "All of the guest rooms are available. You have your pick."

"Where is everyone?"

He reached the top of the landing and turned toward her. His expression registered concern. "You didn't know?"

"Know what?"

"The senior Bishop's are deceased. The Missus went first about eight years ago and then Mr. Bishop last year. The sisters, Celeste, Mavis and Eleanor all married and moved to England. They've never come back, not even for the funerals. Very sad. Just Mr. Bishop left here now."

Ann Marie didn't know what to think. Terrance, here, alone in this rambling house with nothing to keep him company but the memory of a missing wife, dead parents and estranged sisters. It was hard to imagine. But she had a gut feeling he still kept his bed warm.

"What about the other servants?"

"Just me and cook. No need for a full staff. So, which room will it be?"

She looked up and down the winding corridor. "I'll take me old room," she said, walking toward the familiar door.

Marshall hurried in front of her and opened the door. Ann Marie was immediately tossed back in time. The room was exactly as she remembered: the white area rug on the hardwood floors, the terrace that looked out onto the pounding waves, sheer white curtains that danced in the lazy afternoon breeze, bamboo seating with overstuffed white pillows. The entire room emitted a feeling of cool tranquility.

She spun toward Marshall. "Yes, I'll stay here."

He placed her bags in the room. "If you need anything..."

"I'm sure I'll be fine."

He nodded and walked out, closing the door gently behind him.

Ann Marie crossed the room and flung open the terrace doors. She walked out and leaned on the wooden balustrade. Her eyes languidly scanned the beauty that stretched as far as one could see. She drew in a long, cleansing breath, shutting her eyes as the air filled her lungs. Oh, how she missed home. Missed running along the beach, the hustle and bustle of the fish market, picking sugar cane and breaking open coconuts to suck out the milk, letting it dribble down her chin. And the mangos! Ahhh. She could almost taste the sticky sweetness.

"I knew you would pick this room."

Ann Marie gasped in surprise and spun around. "Where ya manners? Never 'eard of knockin'?"

"You're right. I should have knocked." He stood beside her on the terrace. "I apologize." He pressed his hand to his chest. Ann Marie rolled her eyes in response. "Lunch is on the patio out back. Will you join me?"

She looked into his eyes and for an instant she saw a handsome, charming, sexy suitor, who had the uncanny power to dampen her panties with just a look and quicken her heart with a smile. Not the man she'd flown across time zones to divorce.

"In a minute."

"Good. I'll wait…downstairs." He walked out.

Ann Marie stood with her back pressed against the terrace railing. How was she going to get through the next two weeks…in the same house with that man?

Chapter 24

Barbara massaged Victoria's hip in steady up and down strokes.

"You just walked out of his house and he didn't come after you?"

"No," Barbara said. She confessed her tale to Victoria, whom she'd come to regard more as a surrogate mother than one of her patients. "I don't know what to do now."

"Humph, there's nothing for you to do. You made the first move. The next one is up to him. That was a helluva lot to shove down someone's throat."

"I know. I'm not sure what I was expecting."

"I'm still surprised you had the balls to go over there. But then again, if you could throw up your legs right on the massage table, I'll never put anything past you again." She chuckled.

Barbara winced. For a woman pushing her eighties, Victoria was as scandalous as she could be. If nothing, she was refreshing and had no qualms about saying whatever was on her mind. She was a true free spirit.

"So it's really over between you and that young boy, huh?"

"Yes. It's over."

"Shame. He was a real cutie pie. Bet he taught you a few things."

Barbara's thoughts flashed briefly to the torrid episodes with Michael. There were definitely some things she'd learned and things she'd miss.

"Hope you kept that damned ring. It was a beaut."

"I didn't want to. But he refused to take it back."

"Good. A woman never knows when she might hit hard times. And it always makes a good diversion when you don't want to be bothered by the opposite sex."

She'd never thought of it that way. "I guess you're right."

Victoria slowly turned over on the table. "Why are you sounding so down?"

Barbara swallowed. "In a span of a week I've had sex with my ex, broken off my engagement, hurt two wonderful men and wound up alone."

"And who ever said that life was over after forty!" She chuckled merrily.

Barbara shook her head. She had that right.

"Things will get better. They always do," Victoria consoled.

Barbara certainly hoped so.

Wil spent a sleepless night going over everything Barbara told him. At first he'd been so angry, so hurt by what she'd said. The idea that she didn't think enough of him to tell him the truth and believe that he would have stood by her side no matter what, hurt him immeasurably. She thought she was saving his career. The cruel joke was that he never made it to the NFL anyway.

He continued along his mail route, dropping off letters and packages by rote. He shouldn't have let her walk out like that. He should have stopped her. But his emotions were too raw, the information too much to process at the time. Now, thinking it over, his heart softened. She didn't do it out of selfishness; she'd done it because she'd loved him.

Yet, that wasn't all of it. She'd been engaged to another man and she'd made love to him anyway.

That was a fact that he couldn't quite shake off. Did she still care for him as she'd admitted? Was it really over between her and that guy? Was there a chance that he and Barbara could rekindle what they'd once shared?

He knew from the moment he saw her again that his feelings for her had not died all those years ago. And when he made love to her he was certain of it.

Why couldn't life ever be simple?

He dropped off the last of his deliveries and headed back to the station. They needed to talk, without recriminations. He needed to get some things off his chest as well, and then…well, they'd have to see if there was any truth in second chances.

Barbara arrived at the spa around seven. Now that they were fully staffed, her major role was primarily supervision or catering to her special clients. She had one client scheduled for the evening and then she was going home and straight to bed.

"You're moving kind of slow today," Elizabeth said as Barbara approached the reception desk.

"Just a little out of it." She sat down on the stool.

"What's wrong?"

"What's right?"

"Oh you mean about Wil?"

Barbara nodded. "I feel so awful."

Elizabeth patted her hand. "It will work out one way or the other. But in the meantime you can't let your whole world come to a grinding halt."

"I know. It's just hard." She looked into the eyes of her dear friend. "I still love him, Ellie." An ache twisted her insides. "I did so many things wrong."

"No you didn't. You did what you thought was right, for him. Don't blame yourself."

"He had a right to know."

"Maybe he did. But it doesn't change anything and beating yourself up about it won't change anything either."

"He didn't even try to stop me when I left."

"When you left?"

"I went to his house." She told Ellie that she'd taken the girls' advice a step further and went to see him, telling him everything.

Elizabeth listened, aching silently for her friend. "If he's half the man you say he is he'll come looking for you Barb. And if not, your conscience is finally clear."

Barbara sniffed hard. "I guess you're right." She started to get up. "Well, I better get myself together. I have a client in a half hour."

"Don't look now, but I think opportunity just walked through the door."

Barbara turned and her heart stood still. Wil

spotted her and came toward her, his expression unreadable.

He nodded at Elizabeth then turned immediately toward Barbara. "Can we find somewhere to talk?"

"Uh, sure." She threw a glance at Elizabeth.

"I'll get someone to cover for you."

"Thanks." To Wil, she said, "we can talk in the office." She led the way.

"Please, sit down," she said once they were inside.

"I think I'll stand."

Her shaking legs would not give her the same luxury. She took a seat behind the desk. Wil paced in front of her, his head lowered.

"I've been doing some thinking and a lot of soul searching since...I saw you last." He drew in a breath and faced her. "The bottom line is...I still love you. I'm still hurt but finally knowing the truth is easing the pain. We're not kids anymore. We don't have a lot of opportunities to make mistakes and I know letting you walk out of my life would be a major one."

"What are you telling me," she asked, her heart racing with a glimmer of hope.

"I want to try. I want us to be together but only if you're sure it's what you want."

Barbara jumped up and ran to him, stopping inches away. "Yes, yes I want to try."

He pulled her tightly to him, crushing her in his arms. He kissed her hair, stroked her back, murmured words of love in her ear before capturing her lips.

Her soul soared like a bird held too long in captivity then finally set free. All the years, all the trials, all the mistakes were to prepare her for this moment. Second chances do happen and she was determined to make it work.

"You've got to promise me one thing," he whispered against her mouth.

She looked up into his eyes that reflected the happiness in her soul. "Anything."

"You'll never keep the truth from me, no matter what."

"Promise. And you have to promise me something, too."

"What's that?"

"You'll never let us spend another night unsure of what's in the other's heart."

A smile tilted the corners of his wide mouth. "Promise." He kissed the tip of her nose. "How about a personal massage later on to seal the deal?"

Barbara giggled. "Be at my place at ten. I'll make you think you've landed in heaven."

"Now that's an offer that I'd be a fool to refuse."

Reluctantly she stepped out of his arms and instantly missed his warmth. She went to the desk and wrote down her address on a piece of spa stationery and handed it to him.

He looked it over and stuck it in his pants pocket. "How did you know where I lived, anyway?"

She gave him a sneaky smile. "Looked up all your information on our computer."

He chuckled and shook his head. "Technology."

"It's a wonderful thing, ain't it?"

Chapter 25

Ann Marie was pleasantly surprised and a bit disappointed that Terrance didn't try to overwhelm her with charm while they shared lunch. If anything, he was the perfect gentleman, bringing her up to date on the changes on the island and the deaths of his parents. She was moved by the sound of longing in his voice when he spoke of them.

"I didn't realize that I would miss them as much as I do, especially my father." He gazed off into the distance. "Many nights I wish he was around to tell me what to do."

"I can't imagine anyone telling you what to do,

not even Cyril Bishop." She laughed lightly, remembering the towering presence of Terrance's father.

Terrance chuckled. "So, tell me about you, Mari. What has your life been like all these years?"

What could she honestly say; that she'd spent the first five years in the States terrified that he'd find her and show up at her door, the next five burying her hurt in one man after another and the next shutting out the daughter that only made her think of him?

"I found my niche in real estate," she said instead, treading along safe territory. She flashed him a sheepish look. "Something I learned from you and your father." Cyril had been an astute businessman with a keen eye for making a profit on land purchases and development. His son took after him. There was a small Parrish on the island that was owned solely by the Bishop family.

"I always said you were a quick study."

"I own my place as well as an apartment building and I'm co-owner of the spa."

"You've done well for yourself. I knew that you would."

The comment surprised her. "Did you?"

He wiped his mouth with the white linen napkin and placed it down on the table. "There isn't a day that has gone by since you left that I haven't thought of you. At first I was furious to think that you'd actually had the gall to leave me. Me, the great and powerful Terrance Bishop." He leaned back in the chair and chuckled. "You made quite the ass of me." He cocked a brow and looked at her. "I had no choice but to make up for that with every woman I could get my hands on. Prove my manhood, you see."

"Not much different then when we were together."

He flinched at the barb. "It was different. Those women...while we were together...was just something that men do." He frowned thinking back to those days. "But when you left me, the women weren't just silly diversions, they were objects to vent my loss, fill the gaps that you left."

Ann Marie couldn't believe what she was hearing. Terrance had never so much as given a damn about her once she had that ring on her finger and now he was proclaiming the angst of his loss.

"I can tell from your expression that you don't believe me."

"Can you blame me? You made my life with you hell. Not a day went by that I wasn't miserable, hoping, praying that you'd finally look at me, love and honor me as you said you would on our wedding day." She stood abruptly. "It never happened. The only time you seemed to know that I existed was to pleasure yourself. God how I prayed that if I loved you hard enough, gave all of myself to you with you inside me you'd love me back. But you didn't. And I couldn't take it anymore."

"I'm sorry, Mari. I'm sorry for everything." He came around the table and grabbed her arms. "I was a young, arrogant fool. I was too blind to see what I had right in front of me and I took advantage of your love." He pulled her close and she could feel the jerk of his erection. "Let me make it up to you. Give me a chance these two weeks. That's all I ask. Everyone deserves a second chance. Please."

She'd never, in all the years she'd known him, heard him beg. But he was begging now. What would life be like with Terrance now? Had he really changed? Was he now the man she'd wished he had been so many years ago? And what about Sterling?

"Two weeks. Not a second more," she finally conceded and was filled with a sudden sensation of excitement.

The magic of his smile drew one from her.

"You won't regret it. I promise." His gaze held hers even as she held her breath waiting for his kiss.

He released his hold and stepped back. "I have some business to attend to at the office. Why don't you relax, maybe take a swim and I'll be back in time for us to have dinner together." He traced the curve of her jaw with the tip of his finger. "How does that sound?"

She swallowed over her disappointment. "Fine. A swim sounds good."

"I soon come back," he said, reverting to their homeland dialect.

She nodded as she watched him walk away. Slowly she sat back down. He'd done it again, she realized. He'd waltzed right into her heart, the hell with the walls she'd erected. And like the unsuspecting warrior, she'd let the Trojan horse right through the gates.

Ann Marie spent the rest of the afternoon getting reacquainted with the house, finding everything much the same as she'd left it. She wandered to the back of the house and up to where the master suite was tucked away. The balcony door was open. Hesitant, she stood in front of it. On the other side she knew the memories would assault her. This was the room that she and Terrance had shared as man and wife. The bed she given up her virginity on, learned the ways of love on, delivered their daughter on.

She inhaled deeply, pulled the doors open and walked inside. The specially made king-size mahogany bed dominated the room. The canopy rose to the ceiling, the draping so sheer it was almost ghostlike. The white wood floors gave the expansive room the feeling of being in a beach bungalow, but the lavish decor belied the simple flooring. Every piece in the suite had been hand crafted to Terrance's specifications, and assembled in the room, the pieces being too big to get through the doors.

Of course everything shone to a high gloss and the room was so immaculate you would think no one ever entered. But she inhaled Terrance's scent, saw a shirt of his casually tossed across the back of the white wicker rocking chair. She strolled in, running her hand along the smooth surfaces. She opened the closet and found the rows of his clothes lining the racks. Turning, she walked over to the nightstand, drawn by the framed photograph.

She could hardly believe her eyes. She reached out and picked it up, captured by the image of her and Terrance on their wedding day. God, they looked so incredibly happy, so young and carefree. It was the happiest day of her life. She had such high hopes for her future as Mrs. Terrance Bishop.

Why did he still have the picture next to his bed? She'd shoved hers to the bottom of a forgotten box somewhere. Had he resurrected it because he was so sure she would come back and eventually find it? Or had it remained in place all these years?

She put the picture back down. She didn't know what to think. Terrance had systematically broken down every ugly image she'd conjured up about him since he reentered her life. When she left the States she'd been certain about one thing—she wanted to get her divorce and come back home. Now she wasn't sure of anything.

She left the room as quietly as she'd arrived. Maybe that swim would clear her head.

The next few days were a whirlwind of activity. Terrace had put in for time off so that he could spend his days with her. They swam, sailed on his boat; they danced at night and shared intimate dinners on the beach. They laughed and talked deep into the night, often until the sun crested over the horizon. She looked forward to seeing him every day and felt sadly empty when he was not around.

She was being courted by a master, seduced every which way but loose. She knew it but was unable to stop it and to make matters worse, she wasn't sure if she wanted to.

One morning during her second week, she was sitting out front on the veranda reading the local paper when she ran across an article and a picture of Terrance. She set her coffee cup down and read the details. It appeared that Terrance Bishop was running for elected office— Governor General. He'd have jurisdiction over police, judicial and public services. His competition Clive Fuller had challenged him to an open Town Hall debate to discuss the issues. Mr. Fuller was pictured in the article with his wife and two children.

Absently, Ann Marie put the paper down. Why hadn't he said anything to her?

"Here you are." Terrance opened the screen door and stepped out, bare-chested and gorgeous in the morning light. His white cotton pajama pants hung low on his hips and she could almost see the outline of his body beneath when the light hit the pants the right way. His stomach was as tight and firm as a man half his age. She drew her eyes to his face.

"Why didn't you tell me?"

"Tell you what?"

She picked up the paper and pointed to the article.

The corner of his mouth jerked for an instant. "I'd planned to when the time was right."

"What are you talking about?"

He strolled over to the table, pulled out a chair and sat down. "I wanted you to get a chance to know me again."

She frowned. "What does that have to do with anything?" She didn't like the way the conversation was going.

He ran his tongue across his bottom lip. "I have every intention of winning this election. I've poured plenty money into my campaign. Fuller is an asshole. But he has something I don't have."

"What's that?"

"A family."

She jerked back.

Terrance leaned closer. "Politicians are family men. Folks trust family men." He shrugged his right shoulder. "They figure if a man can do good by his family and take care of them, he will do the same for his constituents."

Her stomach rolled.

"I want you and Raquel by my side. My wife and daughter." His eyes lit up as if they'd been set on fire. "We'd have my family money, government money and power! I'd give you whatever you wanted. Anything." He grabbed her by the wrist. "I can win. We can win."

"Now it's all making sense," she said slowly. "This was the real reason why you wanted me back. It had nothing to do with still wanting me." She pointed to the center of her chest. Her throat burned. "What a fool." She sadly shook her head.

"Listen to me. I can give you anything you want. Anything!"

"Anything but you, Terrance. Nothing has changed, least of all you. You're still the same self-centered, egotistical man I knew twenty-odd years ago. The great reconciliation would have won you all the votes you needed. You knew that when you sought me out." She tossed her head back and laughed an empty, nasty sound. She looked him square in the eye. "Not with my help." She pushed back from the table. "Tomorrow morning, I'm going into town to the court office and file the papers. Don't even try to stop it or I'll make sure that everyone who cares will know what you tried to pull…and how you failed. I wonder what your voters will think of you then." She spun away.

Terrance leaped up. "You owe me!"

Ann Marie whirled toward him, her face a hard mask of determination, each word laid out one by one like a poker player with the winning hand. "I don't owe you shit!" She stormed inside, slamming the door so hard it rattled on its hinges.

She ran up to her room and started tossing her belonging in her suitcases as fast as her hands could move. She had to get out of there before she exploded. *Idiot. You stupid fool. You should have known better. But once again, you let that* thing *that he does to your heart and body cloud your mind.* It was over now. Finally and forever over.

Ann Marie spent the next week making sure that all the paperwork was properly filed and that Terrance was officially served. The lawyer she'd secured assured her that he would handle everything in her absence. Since she was not interested in any property and there were no custody issues, he was confident that the process would now be a speedy one.

With that behind her Ann Marie prepared to go home. It had taken her the better part of her adult life to finally see and accept Terrance for who and what he was and to let him go—exorcize him from her spirit.

She was finally free. And whether Sterling was waiting for her return was important but she knew she would survive even if he wasn't. She finally realized that she had been unable to receive and accept real love because she'd never allowed herself to love who she was, to bloom fully into the woman that deserved to be cared about totally. She'd been trapped and stymied by a fantasy. But she'd seen through it and she was ready to step out into the real world—come what may.

Chapter 26

"You're looking mighty happy today," Elizabeth said as Barbara breezed into the spa.

"I am happy." She plopped down on the stool and dropped her backpack at her feet. She propped her elbows on the counter. "Wil and I talked. About everything, and we're going to make it work."

Elizabeth beamed. "Oh girl, I am so glad for you. How often do we get a chance to rekindle our one true love?"

"I know. And to think I was really going to marry Michael." She shook her head. "It's not that I didn't really care about him," she qualified, "but there was always something nagging me in the back of my mind."

"Best to find out now than after you say I do."

"You know that's right."

"At some point you are going to have to formally introduce him to us for the final seal of approval," she said with a raised brow.

"Definitely. But I want to give us some time first." She looked around. "Business is booming as usual, I see."

"That's for sure, and now with the Pause Man contest in full force we're at capacity. I had to actually turn a few men away."

"Who would have thought things would turn out so well."

"As a matter of fact Stephanie is supposed to bring Terri Wells over this evening before we close to pick up the applications from the entries we're received."

"Great, I'm eager to meet her. Stephanie talks about her like she's the second coming."

They laughed.

"Wonder how Ann Marie is making out," Elizabeth said.

"I haven't heard a word from her since she left."

"Me neither. She should be coming home either tonight or tomorrow."

"I sure wish I could have been a fly on the wall."

"You and me both. Anyway, how many do I have for today?"

Elizabeth checked the schedule. "Just one. Kayla and Sheryl are doing an excellent job. We've gotten a lot of compliments from the guys."

"Any feedback from them on how the clients like the new Carol's Daughter products?"

"Actually, what I did was design a comment card. I've been giving them to everyone who goes in for a massage." She reached beneath the desk and pulled out a box and deposited it on the desk "This is just the first box."

Barbara's eyes widened. "Wow." She fished around in the box. "All good I hope."

"From the ones that I went through, they seem to really like it."

"Looks like Stephanie hit another homerun in hooking up with Terri and getting the products in here."

"Yep."

"Well," Barbara stood and stretched, "I'd better get myself settled." She grinned at Elizabeth. "Wil and I are planning a late dinner," she said in a con-spiratorial whisper.

Elizabeth winked. "Don't forget to eat…dinner that is."

Barbara waved her hand and chuckled. "You are so bad."

The first thing Ann Marie did when she returned to her condo was to locate the phone number that Raquel had given to her. She sat down on the side of the bed, picked up the phone and dialed. Raquel answered just as her machine kicked in.

"Hi, Mom. You're back. Hang on a sec. Let me turn off the machine." There was a series of clicks. "Okay. Sorry about that. So, how did it go?"

Ann Marie took her time and told Raquel everything that had transpired while she was under Terrance's spell, right up to the minute the spell was broken.

"I…don't know what to say. I'm so sorry."

"Nothing for you to be sorry about. Me and your dad are both grown ups. One thing…I kept you from your father for years, for my own reasons and that was wrong. No matter what, he's still your father and if you want to work on a relationship with him don't let what happened between him and me stop you."

"I think all I wanted all these years was just to know. I felt as if there was a missing link in my life and if I found my father it would make everything better."

"And now?"

She breathed heavily. "Funny thing about that old saying…"

"What's that?"

"Be careful what you wish for."

They both laughed softly in perfect understanding.

"Hey, why don't you stop by my new place? I'll fix dinner."

"Can I take a rain check? Maybe tomorrow night. There's something I need to take care of."

"There's a Ms. Dennis here to see you."

Sterling's stomach muscles flinched as he listened to his secretary through the speakerphone.

"Should I send her in? She doesn't have an appointment."

His jaw clenched. "Send her in." He adjusted his tie and schooled his expression just as the door opened.

For an unsteady moment, Ann Marie stood stock still in the doorway, uncertain of her reception.

Slowly Sterling stood up. "Come in," he said, his tone devoid of any emotion

Ann Marie lifted her chin and walked inside.

She took a seat opposite his desk and rested her purse on her lap.

"You look well," he said, his voice cool and detached.

"So do you."

"What can I do for you? More legal advice?"

Ann Marie took the barb in stride. "No, my legal troubles are behind me now."

The briefest hint of surprise registered in Sterling's eyes. He cleared his throat. "Glad to hear that," he said, noncommittal. "Well, since I'm a lawyer and you no longer have legal issues, I'm really not sure what I can do for you."

"I didn't sleep with him," she blurted out, wanting to get this game they were playing out of the way. "My divorce is in process and I'm done—finally."

"I see."

She drew in a breath. "I know you don't understand, but it was something I had to do. I had to get it all out of my system once and for all. So that I could live, Sterling. So that I could love…you."

He blinked. Turned his head away for a moment then looked at her. "How can you be sure?"

"Because I finally understand what love isn't." It's not a memory or a hope or wishful thinking. It's about truth and hard times and comfort and being there for each other. It's about wanting the best for someone else so much that you're willing to sacrifice yourself to make sure they have it. It's about realizing that without that person you're not whole." She leaned forward, her eyes pleading with him. "I want to be whole."

Sterling stood up and came around the desk. He stood over her. "Are you sure about this love thing?" Happiness danced in his eyes.

"Very," she whispered gazing up at him. Her heart hammered in her chest.

He stretched out his hand and pulled her to her feet. With his free hand he pressed the intercom, his eyes never leaving Ann Marie's face. "Christine, I'll be out of the office for the rest of the day." He looked at Ann Marie and in slow motion he lowered his head until his lips burned down on hers. He kissed her long, deep and so very slow, locking her body tightly against his.

He didn't realize how afraid he was of losing her until this very moment. He'd steeled his emotions, hoping to shut her out fearing that she may not come back, at least not to him. And he didn't know how he would deal with that. She wasn't like the other women he'd been with—the hit and runs. She carved out a place for herself in his soul and all those years of running around, playing the field was only preparing him. He'd been unable to find or experience real love before and now he knew why. He'd been saving all his loving for her.

Reluctantly he eased his hold on her, but not fully. He tilted up her chin, letting his gaze roam across her face. Her warm brown skin looked flushed, her eyes sparkling, her lips plump. "Why don't we go try out this love thing?"

"There's nothing I'd like better."

Two weeks later.

The hit single *He Is,* by songstress Heather Headley played in the background.

"Sing it girl," Stephanie shouted, raising her bottle of beer in the air.

"Pass the chicken," Elizabeth said, holding out her plate. Barbara forked out two pieces and put them on her plate.

"This was long overdue," Ann Marie said, leaning back against the couch cushions.

"We sure have a lot to celebrate," Barbara said, taking a forkful of salad.

Elizabeth held up some papers in her hands. "It's final! I am officially an unmarried woman. Now Ron and I can sin with smiles on our faces."

The girls whooped with joy.

"Amen and good riddance," Ann Marie said. "Mine is on the way. Hopefully by the time me and Sterling get back from Antigua it will be in my mailbox."

"And when are we going to meet the new...well, old man in your life?" Stephanie asked Barbara.

"Soon, soon. After we get back from our getaway weekend." She grinned wickedly. "He may be old in age but he sure makes up for it with experience!"

They all slapped five and roared with laughter.

"Well I'm tying up my loose ends too," Stephanie announced. "I took out the order of protection against my boss and his nutty wife as you know. But...I'm going to go ahead with the sexual harassment suit." She heaved in a breath. "I need to do it. No matter how it turns out."

"Good for you!" Barbara said. "And you know we're behind you one hundred percent."

"And you're really going to take on Terri Wells as a partner, huh?" Elizabeth asked.

Stephanie nodded. "I know we will make a great team. And I'll never have to worry about being sexually harassed again." She chuckled.

"You think she'll fit in with our quartet?" Barbara asked, tongue in cheek.

"Can she cook?" Elizabeth asked.

"Can she hold her liquor?" Ann Marie wanted to know.

"Does she have a man is the real question?" Stephanie added.

They all looked at each other.

"We sure have plenty to choose from at Pause," Barbara said, surprising them by breaking her own cardinal rule.

"You know our new security guard Drew Hawkins ain't half bad," Elizabeth said.

"But what about that guy who came in the other day..."

"Chile, hush!"

Barbara sat back and listened to the good-natured banter. Ann Marie had finally found Sterling, the man for her. Elizabeth had bloomed since she left her husband and found Ron. Stephanie was on her way to what was sure to be a booming business with her man Tony by her side. And she had Wil, the love of her life.

Now they were going to open their arms, and possibly their hearts and their secrets, to a newcomer. Only time would tell how it would all turn out. But the ride was worth the price of admission.

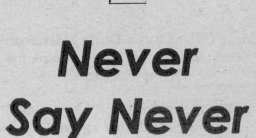

Chase Dillard broke Laura Masterson's heart when he left her to pursue his Olympic dreams.

Winning her love won't be so easy the second time around!

HERE

and

NOW

Michelle Monkou

AVAILABLE JANUARY 2007
FROM KIMANI™ ROMANCE

Love's Ultimate Destination

Available at your favorite retail outlet.

Visit Kimani Romance at www.kimanipress.com.

KRMMHN